Resuscitation of Conflict

C.J. Gowell

ISBN: 978-0-646-72567-3

First published in 2025

Wordpress: https://cjgowellbooks.wordpress.com/

HEADS UP:

This book is entirely a work of fiction. Any characters and events that take place are entirely made up. Any events that happened in the real world, and people exist, are entirely a coincidence.

WARNING: This book contains heavy topics of violence, brief suicide topics, and brief themes of terrorism. Victims of violent actions and suicide ideation are advised to read safely.

July 2024
Five and a half months after the
establishment of Messland…

PERMANENTLY SEALED

Cherilym Offices is a booming company, but it wasn't always like this. Despite the collapse of Belgium two months prior, and the fact the economy had effectively restarted, it had expanded considerably well, even for a start-up. This facility was home to three businesses, all operating within one building: The mobile network F-Reception, a storage company named Funyiers United, and the ever-successful mining business, Stones '4' Us.

Messland, formerly Belgium, is home to its new capital city, known as Cherilym. This city was built on top of the ashes of Brussels. The ones who lost everything in the riots were able to find jobs at the office building in the new city. There were around 70 people working in the one building alone. The other former citizens of the fallen nation had either fled, committed suicide, or were killed in the riots, which dramatically reduced the population of Messland as a whole. The office building was formed by people who had nothing, with the goal in mind to give people job opportunities, one position opening at a time. It was located in the heart of the city of Cherilym, just across the street from the national garden.

Brussels, the original capital city of Belgium, doesn't exist anymore. Rioters spilt throughout all of the streets. It wasn't hard to see why either. In 2023, the year the nation collapsed, the riots got to a destructive standpoint rather quickly. The clinically insane, the pyromaniacs, and the restless all flooded the streets of the once flourishing city. Many rubbish bins were set alight, windows were shattered to the ground, car alarms sounded from all angles, smoke and ash filled the sky, fumes were the only thing that could be smelt, etc. Tensions and civil unrest were beyond high. Belgium was doomed. The fate of the city was sealed: anarchy. Pure anarchy. The thick, smog-filled air, combined with sparks of flames coming from the crowded street created a genuinely apocalyptic feel. All that could be heard was the sound of chanting and car alarms. It was inevitable: Belgium was, by all accounts, going to collapse.

Audible, on the radio, and on television screens, played the national anthem of the shattered state. On the radio, that was all that could be heard, no matter what station someone was tuned in to. Even stations that ceased to exist were brought back by the state for the purpose of playing the national anthem. On the TV screen, however, it was either the National Anthem of Belgium with either text that read "the end," or just the lonely look of static. To the misfortune of the nation and its citizens, this was the end.

The economy, on top of the unstable government, was

not in a good place either. Society in the collapsed Belgium, while in a bad place, was just as bad as the economy. The Government had the idea that printing money in mass would help fix poverty rates in the country, neglecting the fact that other nations in past fell to hyperinflation, such as Germany and Zimbabwe. However, due to the bad logic, prices for pretty much everything went up. From food, to drinks, to petrol, housing, and even children's sweets. Nothing was safe from inflation. Nothing.

October was one hell of a month. The most violent month in the history of Belgium since World War Two, and now the nation was going to collapse. 2024 happened, and the remaining citizens had formed Messland. But the worst was yet to come.

THE WORST WAS YET TO COME

James awoke from his sleep. The bright early morning sun shone through his unclean windows. Due to the former government collapsing, most citizens never recovered – about 90,000 citizens who survived worked through the economic struggles, even if most lived pay check-to-pay check. In contrast, the others who survived the riots (i.e. those who did not commit suicide, get murdered, or didn't flee the country) were below the poverty line. These people lived in poorly constructed and barely furnished homes, with conditions that were potentially comparable to before the Industrial Revolution.

He stood in front of his fireplace, which was placed just under the massive gap in his ceiling, the best infrastructure James had managed to get access to. His house had a bed made from only a wood slab in the corner, a fireplace around the middle of the house (under where the gap was), filthy windows, a floor made of loam soil, and the closest thing you could call to a roof. James' house stood out in the city of Cherilym – it was one of the poverty-ridden houses that was mostly built. The man let out a contented sigh before he slipped on his shoes and sprayed on a can of deodorant. This can was badly burned, and retrieved from the apartment James used to live in before his apartment caught fire during the devastating protests.

James had short brown hair, brown eyes, slightly pale skin, thin and long eyebrows, and was a bit on the scrawny side, all things considered. He always wore plain white t-shirts, jeans, and light grey running sneakers. James was the type of guy to be depressive and have a severe alcohol problem, except he could not drink alcohol at all – he was poor. His job did not do him wonders either – he could barely afford to pay the bills on some weeks. The only good thing is that he at least had warmth, even if the warmth wasn't too reliable.

Before he left, he opened his journal and read his recall of what happened during the riot.

Tensions were high, and the air was hard to breathe. Over the horizon, nothing else could be heard but thunderous chanting. Chaos at Brussels, it was a protest. A riot. People were screaming for various reasons – political changes, the devastated economy, Belgium's debt, and the significantly higher taxes. Well, over ten thousand citizens were chanting for at least two of four of those reasons.

My name is James Sproutt. I'm a journalist, recording the events of the Brussels riots of 2023. I'm in the safety of my apartment, watching the riot intently through the window. This riot started seven hours ago. I'm not too sure what to make of this, however, this riot has resulted in absolute chaos, with no sign of stopping any time soon. My bills are extremely high as of right now, and I've seen my friends already fall into homelessness thanks to our government becoming greedy. I don't blame them, though – the debt they've accumulated is downright stupid. They've borrowed just too much, and can't repay. They forgot the golden rule of loans: Never borrow what you can't return. As simple as that rule is, many people just don't follow it, downright.

James let out a heavy-hearted sigh, then kept reading his writing in his head.

Ok, not even thirty minutes later, a car just blew up outside. The loud bang left cracks in the window I'm spectating this riot from, and might lead to the destruction of this apartment building. I, myself, don't have many options right now. Maybe a news website or something would pay me a lot to give them this story. I know a journalist named Tom. We used to bowl together every Friday until we both found out we both love writing. Ever since then, we've been proofreading and editing each other's various works. I haven't seen him in a while. Maybe he's down there, in the riot crowd. I know he's been affected severely by the bills, having to sacrifice a lot of freedom just to stay on the surface. I don't blame him. I'd be very upset if this was my life too, having to sacrifice my humanity to stay alive.

I had to evacuate the apartment room due to the building catching fire. The car that blew up was caught in flames, which set the building on fire. Smoke and fumes spilt throughout the air, and I experienced the misfortune of breathing all that in. I didn't realise until I could smell smoke. I'm in the safety of the park now, a bit far from the hall. Though I no longer have to worry about being in immediate danger, I can still hear the protestors chanting. It's only a five-minute walk from what was my apartment to the park, after all. Leaving nearly everything behind, I only had enough time to grab my phone, journal, pen, and some money. I could not have expected much, however. It's a bloody riot after all. Any riot is bound to end in something being blown up, a riot is simply not complete without one.

Over the horizon, I can hear sirens blaring. Belgium is now in total anarchy, and all I can do is watch as my home country is destroyed, and falls, before my very eyes. I am not ready. I'm going to go find a new place soon. I don't know where don't know when. I think Cherilym has a place there. I know it's always peaceful in Cherilym. Maybe I'll find a job and get back on my feet in that city. Until then, I'm effectively on the run.

And that was that. With a heavy sigh, James closed his journal, slid it into his backpack, and stepped out of his house.

WORK

Outside of his house, a light drizzle of rain had started
to come down. It wasn't pouring, but it wasn't sprinkling
down either. James left his small house and swiftly paced
from where he lived, down to his workplace. His house was
just around the corner from the office. All he had to do was
turn right from his door, then step down the footpath.
Then make another right turn once more. From there, he
was already at the doors to the building. The scent of the
rain was the only thing he could smell.

Slouching from exhaustion, he made the walk from his
house to his workplace. James worked for Funyiers United.
It was just upstairs the F-Reception, which was upstairs on
the reception floor – his workplace was on floor two. The
man scaled the stairs and made it to his desk, which sat in
the right corner of the left side of the building, just across
from when he came up the stairs. He opened the lid of the
laptop, which was securely bolted to the desk, presumably
to stop theft, He logged in to the company website. From

there, James clocked in, climbed up to the Funyiers United floor, and got to work. The shift he worked consisted of sorting out different things and making sure they were all in the right place. There were always new things to sort out every day, and when he finished, James usually slacked off.

This time, things were different. He had finished sorting things out and laid down on one of the empty shelves, settling in comfortably. Faintly, the sound of keys jingling could be heard coming up the stairs. No mistaking it: this was James' boss. Jingling the keys was something he knew his boss did, whether to show intimidation or just fidgeting. Without any time to spare, he leapt out of the shelf, and with maximum panic, he came up with the bright idea to act like he was working. Like he was working.

Without his skills needing to be pointed out, James' acting just wasn't good – the "acting" consisted of making small humming sounds while staring off into the wall aimlessly. His boss, nicknamed Hugo, picked up the horrible acting skills relatively quickly.

"I see you're practicing for a film, eh?" spoke Hugo. His voice was dripping with sarcasm. "All that acting you're doing, it's stupid really," he spoke with a tone that could only be described as mocking.

Hugo had medium brown hair, swept to the right side. He had unique, bright green eyes. Hugo was slightly taller than James and had an average build. He'd always wear unzipped jackets, a plain t-shirt for an undershirt, jeans, and black leather sneakers. He was the type of guy to appear charismatic on the outside, with those beautifully trimmed eyebrows and smooth, silky skin of his, while looking like he had a major coke problem at the same time. Though, he had no issues with drugs in his life at all.

"Who, me?" asked James, acting oblivious. "I'm just trying to sort out these assets."

Hugo didn't show approval of his antics. He stared daggers at his employee. "Keep this up, and I'm docking your pay. We both know you don't want that," he spoke in a stern tone. "Not in this economy or your position."

James gave a small and sheepish thumbs up and a small soft smile, indicating to Hugo that he got the hint. His boss nodded and left. He took a sigh of relief the moment he was out of view.

When it was time, James stepped downstairs, clocked out of his shift, and went home, reversing the route he followed to get to work earlier that day. He received a few strange looks right his way from other civilians. Standing in his small front yard, James pushed his door open, which lacked a proper lock and key system thanks to his impoverished conditions. Though this wouldn't matter as he didn't have anything worth stealing.

Now in his humble house, James kneeled in front of the firepit. He opened his journal and began to write.

These few months have been hard for me. The gap in the ceiling and the roof was essentially letting the dead cold of the night in. What is there to live for anymore? What is there to love? Is there even such a thing as miracles? I stopped believing in luck a long time ago, when my bills just kept rising back in Brussels, with no sign of stopping.

After a hum of finishing his work, James closed his journal, stood up, and sat on the wooden slab he called a bed. That big block of wood was the closest thing he had to a proper bed. James tossed himself to the "bed" and faced the wall.

"Let me tell you all I can do," spoke a creature. James and the creature were in a dark corridor. It was hard to make out the shape, but looked like a skeleton, deep blue build, and had bright glowing mouth and eyes, and it was starting. Additionally, ice started to form around the corridor, surrounding the helpless man.

"What is happening?" asked James. "Who are you?"

The creature did not talk yet. It floated towards James. It then spoke. "The Wraith."

He woke up, emotionless. A nightmare, all about a weird monster. Nightmares were weird, but this one felt like a typical horror movie if anything. James did not like that. Who would?

Over the next few weeks, work was essentially the same –

clock in, organise stuff, slack off, lunch, go home, and so on. For the £1,200 a week James was given, it was not hard to see that organising things for a living was a decent job (at least in terms of difficulty). To James, it was almost impressive that a job with moderately minimal effort involved like this was even a thing, all during the height of inflation. After the collapse of Belgium. With one-third of the population making the death toll, and the sixth-eighth of the survivors fleeing. Previously, Belgium had 11.6 million. Now remained a rough estimate of 100,000 citizens.

While he slacked off on his job, James reminisced and reflected on everything: his job, the riots, everything. Ever since his life turned around, he had significantly less time to do what he truly cared for: writing. Maybe, someday, James would have a place to go. The feeling of the cold, somewhat air-conditioned building stuck to his skin.

PREPARATIONS

Belarus was worse off than its ally, Russia. It had to deal with more corruption and civil unrest. Because of the unrest, this country was a prime target for terrorists, and it almost always had some sort of terrorist threat targeting the nation. Such threats included kidnappings, sieges, massacres, shootings, and even missile threats. The corrupt state was not in good shape internally either – a government that is, supposedly, unaware of its own corruption (they play dumb to minimise the risk of a riot), civilians who are mostly oblivious to corruption (with some choosing to keep silent to avoid unruly arrest), and sanctions from all angles. Overall, Russia's ally was just a bad place to live in. Though, neither country was good in any sense.

The Leader of Belarus, who went by Vladimir Ivan Grongle, was responsible for the state of his nation (which his administration always played dumb to the effects of). In the past, he'd written an autobiography. In summary, it served as a propaganda tool to make him seem like a glorious leader to his citizens, who acted none the wiser (whether clueless or choosing to play along with the corruption). The leader was ruthless in his rule, and on top of being the president of the horrible nation, he was also the leading judge of the Belarusian Supreme Court. This court was the only court in the nation, and on top of the president being the Leader of both the court, as well as the country entirely, Grongle got to give whatever punishment he saw fit for the convicted criminals in his country, from mere small-time offenders to hardened criminals. Essentially, the ruthless man was an established dictator.

Ivan had blue eyes, a full bald head, a bit on the bulkier side of things, and what was known as a "resting bitch face." He also had a bit of a big nose, and a frown at all times, as well as a charcoal-black suit, black leather shoes, and a blood-red tie (quite literally looked like it was painted with blood). His tone was sharp, and the tyrant that was Ivan Grongle was always straight to the point, never having time for filler when making conversation. Ivan started as a businessman, then transitioned to become a lawyer, and after that, he ended up running to become the leader of Belarus. He was the kind of guy that, by no means, you'd want to annoy if you knew what was good for you.

The midday sun was in full effect, beaming down over the northern nation. The clock mounted on the wall ticked quietly in the background. Ivan sat in his office chair, resting both elbows on the dark wood desk, and rested his hands on his head. Lethargically, he reached for his coffee mug and took a swig. He preferred double-shot coffee. After taking a swig of his beverage, he resumed typing on his computer.

His office was a luxury form of fine, deep wood, with corners and outlines made from solid gold. In his office lay a soft red carpet, a large desk made from a darker shade of wood, and a chandelier made from (again) real gold, with 22 electric candles. The door was perfectly centred and had beautifully frosted glass. You could hardly see through the glass, but it looked exceptional either way you looked at it. In the front corners stood bookshelves on either side, leaving enough room between the door and each bookshelf for a pot plant on either side as well. These pot plants contained lovely geranium plants. In the opposite corners sat pot plants as well, with those plants holding coral bells. Behind Grongle's desk was a massive, frosted window, overlooking the horizon of his nation. It had yellow curtains, which were usually closed. The dictator was paranoid of spies and stalkers.

Ivan's secretary, named Louise, opened the door and stepped into the office. The tyrant looked over at her. A wicked smile formed over his mouth.

"Ah, Louise," spoke Ivan in a condescending tone of voice. "Please, have a seat."

Louise made her way to Ivan Grongle's desk and took a seat in front of him with a stern and numb look on her face.

Being the secretary and spy of a dictator, she had an adamant and no-bullshit attitude.

"Mr President, I've located a known trio of terrorists," she spoke in a firm tone. "One of which was identified to be of Russian citizenship," she continued.

Louise was your average one-of-a-kind secretary. She had blonde hair tied in a bun, the deepest of blue eyes, a serious tone on any occasion, and a purple rose parted to the left side of her head. She looked right out of a spy film.

Ivan looked her dead in the eye. "Do you have a photo of them?" he asked.

She nodded silently and proceeded to pull out four photographs. One of the photos contained what looked like a Russian marine.

"His name is Doomo," she said and slid the photo to Ivan.

The second photo showed a guy in a ghillie suit and a noticeable grenade belt.

"This is Greene," stated Louise, and gave him the photo.

The third photo was a guy in a black suit and helmet, with red outlines and patterns.

"That is Crimson," she said as she slid that one through to the ruthless leader.

"And here's all of them together," she said. Louise passed

over the fourth and final photograph. The fourth photo contained all of them discussing stuff. Crimson was holding a double-barreled pump shotgun, and Greene was holding a grenade launcher.

Ivan nodded and searched through each photo individually. He then placed the photos into his drawer, located to the left of his desk. After sliding the drawer closed, he glared at his secretary dead in the eye.

"And what are their plans?" asked Ivan, as if this were an interrogation.

"I don't know," Louise replied.

He sighed and pinched the bridge of his nose, as if he were checking to make sure he wasn't in a dream. "Just… get these three to me." He spoke in an irritated tone.

Louise nodded and left the office.

"Like, RIGHT NOW!" shouted Ivan, being the hot head he was. Louise was already gone.

LOCATED

Minutes turned to hours, and hours stayed as hours. After five hours, Louise returned with all three of the suspected terrorists, as well as a few bodyguards for good measure.

"Here," she said. The suspected terrorists stepped towards Vladimir Grongle's desk.

Knowing what to do, they all stood in front of the desk. They all raised their hands in the air to indicate that they weren't intending to cause harm. They all got on their knees as well, as if to sell the idea to the dictator that they all weren't a threat to his safety at all.

"All right, you three. Let's start the talk," spoke Ivan. In unison, they all gave the leader their undivided attention. "Ok, Louise, get out of my office."

She nodded and left the office. The two bodyguards remained, standing in front of the pot plants by the door, to make sure that none of them had any chance to escape or threaten the leader's physical safety, not that it would've mattered since they were unarmed. Ivan stood up from his office chair and eyed them.

"Tell me," he spoke in a condescending tone as he looked down at the trio. "Who are you three?"

Crimson was the first to talk. "It's Crimson. The guy in the ghillie suit is named Greene, and the marine in the spy hood is Doomo."

Ivan nodded in satisfaction with the honesty. Then he proceeded to speak. "Good, I knew you guys wouldn't lie." Grongle stood up and paced around the room from the safety of behind his desk. "Not to my face."

Doomo's eyes darted around the room, then he glanced at Crimson, followed by Greene, and then back at Ivan. "So, why'd you get her to bring us into this office?" he spoke.

"Because I want you guys to do something for me," the dictator responded. "I want you guys, with the help of my armed men, to help take Messland off the map."

The three men looked at each other, then shrugged.

"Wait, us?" Greene broke the silence. "Why us?"

Ivan looked toward Greene, frustrated, letting out a sigh, then spoke. "Because you three have shown to be quite capable. My secretary, who's also my spy, has been watching you all, as well as reporting back to me."

Collectively, the trio exchanged glances once more and

collectively raised an eyebrow. All were bewildered.

Crimson opened his mouth to say something, but didn't talk as Ivan continued to speak. "You guys have proven to be unstoppable. Wiping out villages, leaving no survivors, bombing stuff… yeah. Don't you dare assume I'm oblivious to this," he said that last sentence in a harsh, threatening tone.

Crimson was the first to respond. "Don't you have a military?"

Ivan gritted his teeth. "Did I stutter when I said your goodie two-shoes looking ass would be wiping Messland off the map, *along* with my armed men?" he yelled in frustration. "Are you actually stupid?" he continued. "Like, c'mon, at least try to comprehend what I have to say. We speak the same language for fuck sakes."

Crimson gritted his teeth too and looked as though he was about to lash out. However, he chose the smart route to contain himself. Probably for the better, considering he was right in front of the leader of Belarus himself. If Ivan so chose, he'd have his staff turn their heads into decorations.

After they leave the president's house, they exchange looks with each other. They then study the weapons they were given. Crimson was given an AR-15 with no scope, Greene was given a Glock-17, and Doomo was given a bolt-action sniper rifle.

They jump into a jeep, with Doomo being the nominated

driver. "So, to Messland…"

As Doomo got ready to set out, a helicopter pilot stepped in front of the 4x4 wheel drive.

"You three headed to Messland?" he spoke, in a pilot-like tone.

Doomo got out of the car. "Yeah." Crimson and Greene followed behind.

"Well, hop in," said the pilot, and paced toward a helicopter. This helicopter was built for the convenient transportation of soldiers, as established with no visible weaponry to be seen. And so, they climbed into the passenger bay, just behind the cockpit. The driver climbed into the cockpit of the helicopter, starting up the rotary blades soon after.

AIRSPACE

The rotary blades started to spin. Gradually building up the pace, one thing became clear: They were about to launch an attack on Messland. Similarly, multiple other helicopter blades started to spin as well. Behind them, the garage doors opened. Everything from tanks to jeeps was being serviced. They were going to come into the mix later, possibly after the first attack, whatever Vladimir Ivan Grongle had planned.

Doomo's portable radio started to crackle and static, and then a voice replaced that static.

"Can you hear me?" spoke a voice. It was the voice of Vladimir Ivan Grongle himself.

Doomo spoke into the portable radio. "Loud and clear."

Ivan responded. "Your first mission is to bomb the residential streets of Cherilym City." Static. "Then, you need to shoot up the Office building. If you get captured, commit suicide."

Crimson was writing this down on a notepad. They all grimaced at being told to end their own lives if they faced prosecution. Doomo responded with an unstable "got it," then an "over."

"Excellent," spoke Ivan, a hint of malice audible in his tone. "Don't fuck this up."

Then silence.

The helicopter pilot looked behind him to see Crimson, Greene, and Doomo in the passenger bay.

"Are we clear to launch?" he asked.

The three of them glanced at each other and then nodded. "Clear. Ready when you are."

The captain nodded. Soon enough, the helicopter was airborne. Take-off. "You all have code names? For like, missions and stuff?" he asked.

"Oh… no," spoke Crimson, followed by a "nope" from Greene.

"I see… well", the pilot pointed at Crimson. "You're Blazefront."

Then, the pilot pointed at Greene. "You're Mosscrack."

After that, he pointed at Doomo. "Your name is Sharpsnipe."

The pilot then pointed a thumb at himself. "It's Skips, as cliché as that is."

Crimson, now unofficially *Blazefront* for missions, looked Skips dead in the eye. "Very cliché, yeah." Crimson then rolled his eyes, making his annoyance known.

The helicopter flew overhead, first flying over the land of Poland. The pilot's portable radio, mounted next to the GPS, started to crackle.

A male voice with a thick Polish accent spoke.

"This is Poland Air Control. You've been identified as an unknown aircraft. Please confirm your status. Over."

The tone of the male's voice was easily distinguishable. He was not playing around. The mission could very well end before it starts if Skips didn't give a valid explanation in time…

Skips turned on his radio and spoke into it.

"Ground control, this is A1-353. We're headed to Messland from Belarus for military drills. Over."

The male voice replied after a firm three minutes' worth of static. "You're free to continue. Over."

And continue flying over Poland, Skipper did.

"You're good at lying," Crimson chimes in.

Skips laughed. "I wasn't always this good."

"And also," said the Polish voice, "while we were at it, we informed German traffic control. You're clear to fly through German airspace, too. Your fleet of aircraft has been pinged to avoid future confusion. Over."

Pinged. "Clear. Thanks for the assist. Over," spoke Skips, then turned off the radio.

This wasn't a good situation for Skips, Crimson, Doomo, and Greene. They're expected to land in Messland now. But as long as they kept the mission anonymous, it would not matter. Right?

They all flew over Germany, pinged. While it was a good feeling knowing they'd successfully deceived the government, any mistakes and the mission may be compromised. They had to play their cards right, between now and landing in Messland, wherever they end up landing in the new country.

The trip was coming to an end as the helicopter started to descend slowly toward the Earth's surface. They chose to land in a forest, away from Cherilym to avoid suspicion. Deprived of access to the outside world, Crimson, Greene, and Doomo hopped out of the helicopter, weapons readied. The helicopters took off soon after. As they took off, it became clear that the other two helicopters were decoys in case things went south and Plan B needed to be enacted. Plan B was to fight against enemy aircraft in pursuit of them. For the Belarusians, that plan never came to be utilised, and thus, a (mostly) smooth landing.

The trio looked around at their surroundings. A large temple, which was clearly in a state of decay, is visible. Crimson steps closer and feels the heat.

The temple was built a bit like a church, constructed with dark grey and black bricks, with spires on the left and right side of the entrance, the left one out of commission entirely – likely from weather decay. The spires have gold traces on them. Behind the temple – presumably attached to it – was a large structure with lit flames on top of the wall, as well as more traces of gold. This behemoth of a structure looked to be where either cage fighting happens, or if a sleeping deity was resting inside of it.

Crimson stepped away from the temple and turned towards the other members in his squad.

"It's a temple," he said.

Doomo steps towards Crimson. "Well, no shit." He had anger issues.

"All right, let's just do our mission. Then we can fuck out of here," said Greene, then he pulled out his Glock-17. "Seriously, this place does not seem right… It feels like there's something supernatural around here."

Greene was the type of guy to be cautious, albeit a bit paranoid. Especially in foreign environments. However, he always blamed it on his gut feeling, and could never have picked up on paranoia.

Doomo looked toward Greene, picking up on the paranoia he was showing. "You good there?" he asked and raised an eyebrow.

Greene looked at Doomo. "I'm fine. Just…" He took a deep breath. "This temple? It doesn't seem right."

Doomo tilted his head and shrugged. He failed to see the big deal in the temple. The thought was nothing but mere paranoia…The thought of a deity, existing. Sleeping. Living. In the temple. It could not be real.

After traversing the forest for a few hours, they hear the sound of cars travelling. As if driven by instinct, they sprinted towards the source of the noise, and they laid eyes on Cherilym City.

"That looks like the target," said Doomo. "Big, but not huge."

Crimson and Greene nodded as they continued to look at the building. Then, they look at each other.

Doomo stepped between them, then another step, so that he was in front of them, and perfectly centred between them. "You guys," Pause. "Can take this mission."

Crimson and Greene exchanged looks. Then Doomo continued to speak. "Bomb the residential street, then massacre the office… whatever it was named."

Greene put his Glock-17 away, then Crimson held his AR-15 with a firm grip.

BRUISED AND SCARRED

The time was 1:42 pm. James had been at work for a couple of hours now. By now, he had finished sorting out the assets, and now he was slacking off, scrolling through Twitter.

Earlier that week, mobile services came back online, meaning the citizens of Messland could now use the internet. And go online they did, only to find people posting various memes about the collapse of Belgium, as well as people just replying to threads.

James got sick of the repetitive memes quickly. He closed the app and deleted it soon after. After that, he stepped to the other side of the floor and looked out the window. From there, he saw two foreign-looking people he'd never met before: one in a ghillie suit, and one in black and red. The guy in black and red was holding an AR of some kind – James wasn't too sure about the type of weapon it was.

He wasted no time taking out his journal and writing

everything: descriptions of the foreigners, what they were holding, what he assumed their intentions were, and so on.

6:12 pm. James walked back home. He had already turned the corner when…

A low and deep *boom* is heard. The ground beneath his feet shook violently. A few bright and burning spheres of heat expand at a rapid pace. James leapt back onto the road with little time to spare. He had no choice.

He woke up. Fire could be seen everywhere around. James sat up and looked around. His vision was blurry, his movements were weak, and his breathing was shallow. He could not remember anything that had happened. James came to his senses and looked around, then saw his house. The house, that was already due to be destroyed, was. He was devastated. James reached for his journal that he carried under his shirt. It was still there. He let out a sigh of relief. As he sat up, the man's hearing was returning to normal from just being a series of constant ringing.

The ringing in his ears slowly faded away as air raid sirens could be heard in the distance. Whatever happened, it was severe enough to cause something like this.

James retreated towards the alleyway between Cherilym Offices, and the tavern. He slowly paced toward it, injured. Exhausted. Hungry. As he made his way towards the alley,

James felt a weird burning sensation on his arm. He glanced at his arm and saw a nasty 3rd degree burn there, surrounded by a large scrape covered in blood. James only then realised that the blood that had been coming from his messy arm had been coming out since he stood up. He walked from the road to the alleyway between Cherilym Offices and the tavern. Behind him, a long trail of splattered blood. The nasty stinging burn on his arm persisted as silence and smoke filled the air once more.

He slumped down next to a dumpster and attempted to sleep. He could not sleep at all. The stinging pain was too strong for James to fall asleep with. What even was proper sleep?. James had no other option: stay awake until he eventually passed out from exhaustion.

The following morning, he woke up to a car speeding by the alleyway. James looked around, then saw the nasty burn on his arm once more, and a pool of blood on the ground between him and the dumpster. Some of the blood stained his jeans. But the main bleeding had stopped.

"Did I pass out from blood loss?" he slowly asked himself, realising that he had bled quite a bit.

Living in an alleyway was James' life now. A depressing life in an alleyway, with quite possibly a permanent burn on his arm, having to survive off of scraps and rubbish in the bin, with little hope of ever having a stable roof over his head again. And with nobody to turn to, he was effectively alone in this world. Trying to move his arm, even a little bit, would be painful. Even getting up would be a lot to ask for without assistance. When he moved his arm a bit, a large stabbing pain could be felt where his burn was.

"Shit…" seethed James, the curse slipping out from between his teeth.

The homeless man was, now, in the worst spot in his life. Bruised and scarred. And this wouldn't be the last time this happened either. He knew that too well. He could practically taste the lingering terror threat.

Early-August 2024

MASSACRE

Newspapers flew throughout the street, the park, the stands, and in front of the doors of buildings. An attack in Cherilym so soon into the country's formation. The newspapers read:

Attack On Europe – What YOU Need to Know

Presented by Apollo Alltrussi (News Reporter)

An attack in Messland last night left twelve dead, seven missing, and an unknown amount of people injured. Something this had has not happened since the horrific riots that brought Belgium down and beaten the European economy to a pulp.

The attack is assumed to be a deliberate act of terrorism and is actively being looked into. All citizens are being urged to stay away from the explosion zone for the time being, as fumes may cause disorientation, nausea, vomiting, and in the worst case: cancer.

Additionally, a mandatory curfew for all non-essential workers will be enacted as announced by Senator Jeriah early this morning.

What does this mean for you? A good chunk of people living where the explosion happened may just be homeless as we speak. A blood trail from the scene of the crime can be traced to the alleyway, where a survivor now lives on.

Messland will recover. We may not be in a wonderful situation, but we WILL recover from this unforgivable act of terror.

Crimson and Greene waited out behind the newly constructed Cherilym Nature Conserve, which was essentially a small park inside a greenhouse. A path in and out, forming a U-shape, with trees outside of the path, as well as wooden benches. Between the U-shape was a pond, which contained some seagrass, but no fish to be seen.

Greene was holding a map of the city in one hand, and in the other hand was a tipped pen. Crimson looked at the map to see what he was doing.

"What are you doing?" Crimson asked, with a hint of curiosity being audible in his expression.

Greene looked at him and said, "I'm looking for a way to sneak into Cherilym Offices. It's for Part B of the operation. The one where we've been told to massacre."

Crimson nodded and took a peek at what he had done so far. It looked like the only way through was to just go from where they stood now and just cut through the street when not a lot of people would be outside. Due to the state of Cherilym, with not many people out during peak hours (maybe one or two in the public garden), this task would not be too hard to pull off at all. Everyone would be either at work or at home, maybe a few people going for a walk.

1:42 pm. The time had come. The deed had to be done. A massacre in Cherilym Offices. Crimson took a peek outside and saw a civilian walking through the garden's entrance. He shortly dismissed the passerby. Not wanting to cause a scene and sell the mission, he didn't fire.

The garden had many dark grey bricks surrounding it, surrounded by beautiful purple rose bushes, and a smooth cobble path, perfect for biking.

Crimson glanced at his partner and nodded. The time had come: the mission was a go.

Greene took the lead, followed by Crimson, who was loading a mag into his AR-15. The streets were effectively dead. The air was a bit moist, but it was still bright outside. A sunny day with not many clouds in the sky.

The duo arrived at the left door to Cherilym Offices. Greene pulled out a previously prepared lockpick and got to work. The lock was picked, and the door was opened.

"Where'd you get that?" asked Crimson, referring to the pick.

"I always carry one around," Greene replied, then put it

back in his pocket. "Y'know, for shit like this."

"Good to know," his partner replied.

Both of them stepped into the building. The two were met with the scent of fresh lumber and a newly laid-out carpet. The ground floor appeared to be a reception and waiting room, only without a reception desk. Perhaps it was just where breaks happened. There was seating and tables around, and by the front window stood a table.

Earlier, Greene agreed to act as the scout, whereas his counterpart, Crimson, would be the one to kill the employees. He turned the corner and saw someone on top of the table by the window. Crimson followed behind him and spotted the guy. The employee was lying down on the bench. He looked up at the duo and instantly started to panic.

"Please don't shoot!" he yelled, before being cut off by a loud bang from Crimson's AR-15. They noticed blood dripping from his upper jaw. Not long after, he collapsed and bled out.

Crimson and Greene chuckled to themselves as the dead employee rolled off the table and flopped onto the fresh carpet, blood staining the red fabric that made it up. They take a second to regain their composure. The duo climbed up the stairs to the second floor to find the F-Reception mobile phone service department.

That day, only one person was there. Greene stepped slowly toward the preoccupied worker. When he was close enough, Greene punched him clean in the eye. The worker, whose name badge read 'Jeremy,' looked over and saw his attacker.

Jeremy shrieked in fear and confusion. "Who are you? And what do you want?"

"Come with me," spoke Greene, a stern attitude in his tone of voice.

Jeremy reluctantly nodded and stepped out of his swivel chair. He followed Greene to where Crimson was, who was standing by the stairs up to the next floor, the rifle in hand. The active shooter alarm had started sounding. The building was on lockdown.

Jeremy is forcefully stood in a specific place, just two steps away from Crimson, who clutched his AR-15 in a firm grasp. He was ready to fire, assuming Jeremy refused to cooperate with Greene.

"What do you want from me?" shrieked Jeremy in a panicked voice.

Greene took out a box of pills, which had the label from the capsule ripped off. The capsule was transparent and dark green, indicating it was probably used before. It could not be good. He took out a single pill, and Crimson aimed directly at Jeremy's forehead.

"Take this pill and don't say a word," spoke Greene,

before forcing the pill down his throat.

Jeremy choked, but eventually swallowed the pill down. Immediately, he clutched his stomach, and within seconds, he was throwing up violently and gasping for air. His limbs started to feel very weak as he did everything he could to hold on for dear life.

"What the fuck," he spoke in a shallowed whisper. His arm fell right off his torso, prompting him to collapse.

James was still silently suffering in the alleyway he was in, in a severe amount of pain. He'd been listening to everything going on inside his workplace, with no ability to stop what was happening.

The terrorist duo advanced up to the storage facility, where James worked. Because James was not at work, he wasn't in any form of direct danger from the unprovoked attack on his workplace.

Crimson took his place at the stairwell and held his rifle tight. He glanced around the room and discovered there was nobody in his line of sight.

"All right, Greene. Search this floor, and subdue anyone in hiding," he ordered as he checked his mag.

Greene nodded and made his way to the shelving area. But nobody was there. Then he stepped over to the storage compartments. The chests were wooden and opened sideways, like a fridge, except smaller.

One by one, from left to right, he opened each storage chest, checking what was in each compartment. From documents, construction materials, sticks and stones. Some of the documents were just general paperwork. Most of the construction supplies were salvaged from other construction projects before the collapse of Belgium. As for the sticks and stones, they were just there.

Greene spent fifteen minutes searching the Funyiers United floor, discovering nobody was hiding. He stepped back to Crimson.

"Clear," spoke Greene.

"All right," replied Crimson, "All set to go upstairs then."

The duo arrived at the top floor, before the rooftop. They see a ton of different excavated minerals and stones, possibly from a closed mining company from when Belgium was still a thing. Crimson glanced around the room, looking for any potential targets. The door to the stairwell, which led to the rooftop, slammed shut as Crimson set his sights on that door. It was immediately obvious somebody was trying to escape. Dashing up the stairs, the duo gave chase, with the hopes of finding whoever was making an attempt to flee.

Finally, they made it to the rooftop floor and spotted a tanned bald guy, most likely an employee of the mining company. Crimson aimed his rifle at the bald guy, ready to shoot. The bald guy turned around and glanced down at the road below, then looked back at the terrorist duo. Before any shots could be fired, he did the unimaginable.

AFTERMATH

The unnamed bald guy stood over the edge of the building. He leapt backwards. Falling, he had a big, unmistakable grin on his face. Time felt like it slowed down a lot for Crimson, Greene, and the employee to the point where it felt like it had paused altogether.

He hit the road beneath him with a splat. Blood splattered around his body, with the impact of the fall killing him instantly. Time had gone back to normal. The back of his body had become unrecognisable, with blood drenching it. The back of his head looked like it was hit by a fastball, and the fastball went right through to his brain.

A military personnel helicopter landed just outside of the greenhouse. A captain, a sniper, and four other troops flood out.

"Captain Yuri," yelled the sniper over the helicopter blades. "Give the order!"

Captain Yuri nodded and beckoned the squad to follow behind.

"Positions!" yelled Yuri. The squad took their positions. "Jackson, take the greenhouse rooftop!"

The sniper, named Jackson, nodded and made his way to the roof of the greenhouse.

Captain Yuri Katō wore a blue captain's vest, a white undershirt, long brown leather pants, and black heavy-duty boots. He also wore a captain's hat and black gloves. Yuri carried an MP7 submachine gun in his right hand. He was the squad captain of the JSDF.

Jackson Herehshie was Yuri's apprentice. He wore a green singlet, an ammunition belt carrying ammo for rifles, brown leather pants and black leather shoes. He also wore brown fingerless gloves and a green and white striped sweatband. Jackson was a Saudi Arabian working with Yuri in the JSDF. Aki, Kenji, Daichi, and Akio were wearing standard military uniforms, and each of the men was armed with an AR-15 and a Glock-18 pistol.

This squad had been selected after they had demonstrated the ability to shoot well during their days of training. Each soldier took their place. Daichi was standing next to Yuri. The two were in front of the green tavern's front doors as a potential ambush point. Kenji, Akio, and Aki were in front of the nearest garden entrance to Cherilym Offices. They were all trying to ambush the attackers.

Yuri pulled out a portable radio and turned it on.

"Prepare to fire," he ordered.

Crimson and Greene looked over the edge of Cherilym Offices and saw they were surrounded by an armed squad. There'd be no way for them to escape. Not without a distraction…

Greene nudged Crimson's arm and said, "I have an idea."

Crimson looked at him and raised an eyebrow. With noticeable scepticism, he asked, "What's your idea?"

"Follow my lead," spoke Greene. Forcefully, he dragged Crimson towards the other edge of Cherilym Offices. The edge they got closer to was overlooking the tavern and the forest behind it.

"Ready to jump?" asked Greene as he let go of Crimson's arm and leapt towards the tavern's balcony.

"You're insane…" murmured Crimson as he leapt behind, rifle held tightly.

Yuri and Jackson spotted the terrorist duo on the outer patio of the tavern. Jackson aimed at Crimson's head and Yuri passed on the word to the other soldiers, "clear to engage."

"Cover me!" shouted Daichi.

"I got you covered," responded Kenji. He made his way over to Daichi, siding with him.

The front doors of the tavern opened. The moment Greene was in clear view, Captain Yuri ordered fire. Before long, bullets started flying at the tavern's doors. The bullets strike the door ferociously, but they all had missed their target. Crimson and Greene were cornered. They had nowhere to go. It felt as if they had nowhere to go, until…

ESCAPE

Crimson's fingers latched onto his smoke grenade. He pulled the pin and dropped it. Instantly, thick smoke filled the doorway, masking the appearance of the duo entirely. Yuri tried and failed to spot them amidst the fog.

He grabbed a tight hold of his portable radio and yelled into it, "Hold your fire!"

Hearing this, everyone held their guns to the bitumen road, away from the enemy position. Subconsciously, they knew it was to avoid accidentally killing a civilian, if anyone was there at all.

The thick smoke cleared. Crimson and Greene were nowhere to be seen in the tavern. Akio and Kenji immediately stormed the tavern in search of the terrorists. Kenji was the lead, and Akio was to cover for an ambush if it happened.

When they snuck inside, they glanced at a window. It was

shattered. It was the window closest to the front counter. The opening of the smashed window led to the forest that surrounded the outskirts of the city. Kenji and Akio left the tavern and stepped toward Yuri in defeat.

"Find any leads?" Yuri asked, raising an eyebrow.

Kenji nodded. "One of the windows to the left of the building was shattered."

He paused to breathe, and Akio said, "They must have escaped into the woods."

Captain Yuri took this all in, exhaled a breath, and nodded. "Very well," he spoke. He turned his radio back on. "We will fall back and retreat to the Messland Military base," he said into the radio, informing the other squad members who weren't nearby of what was about to happen.

The soldiers in Cherilym regrouped back at the helicopter they arrived in, and Yuri entered the cockpit. Once everybody was inside the helicopter, it took off into the sky.

Mid-August 2024

NOW SHOWING

"Now showing: *The Descent*," spoke an announcer, before the projector flared to life. *The Descent* is a film that was released in 2005. It was about a cave exploration going wrong, the cave being filled with monsters and other unsettling things.

It had been exactly a week since the massacre of Cherilym Offices took place. For trauma coping, civilians inside the city, as well as neighbouring towns, were invited into the tavern to watch films together, talk, and overall have a relaxed, peaceful community-building event. That's how it was supposed to be in the tavern. Though the office building was still closed from the massacre, and likely would not reopen for a long time, if ever. This left the only surviving employee – James – out of a job, with no source of income.

James had healed a bit between the bombing of the　　**"Now showing: *The Descent*,"** spoke an announcer, before the projector flared to life. *The Descent* is a film which was released in 2005. It was about a cave exploration going wrong, the cave being filled with monsters and other unsettling things.

It had been exactly a week since the massacre of Cherilym Offices took place. For trauma coping, civilians inside of the city, as well as neighbouring towns, were invited into the tavern to watch films together, talk, and overall have a relaxed, peaceful community-building event. That's how it was supposed to be in the tavern. Though the office building was still closed from the massacre, and likely would not reopen for a long time, if ever. This left the only surviving employee – James – out of a job, with no source of income.

James had healed a bit between the bombing of the housing and now, being able to move. He had managed to cover his arm with a damp t-shirt, which was helping his distressing injury. He hadn't slept a lot between the events of the explosion and now. Leaning against the wall and watching the movie, this was the best thing that had happened to him since before the riots happened.

The movie ended. Eleven people leave the tavern. All eleven had left a tip of around £2 each behind. It was the least they could do. The fourteen people who stayed continued to chat. The community event was still on, after all. The bartender, a middle-aged man wearing a standard bartender uniform and with hazel eyes and brown hair, put on another film. This movie was titled *'Farinelli.'* Released in 1994, the drama played on the projected wall as everyone continued to socialise.

The time was 5:22 pm. The setting sun crept through the windows as *Farinelli* ended.

"Thank you all for coming," spoke the bartender as he collapsed onto the counter. He was exhausted.

The remaining fourteen people gradually left the tavern. James left as well and went back to the alleyway, which he was now forced to call his home. He leaned against the furthest dumpster from the alleyway entrance. The sun was nearly fully set, and the cool temperatures of the night had already started to sink in.

It was a new day outside. The brightness of the sun's rays shone over James's closed eyes, abruptly waking him up from his slumber. Grudgingly, he groaned and used the dumpster to get up from the ground and start his day.

James had barely eaten any food or drunk any water at all. He could be at risk of death any day now if he does not find anything soon. James stepped onto the streets, which were crowded with people chanting and yelling, with very few police officers trying to calm down the raging crowd.

Swiftly, he came to his senses. It was a riot. James had a flashback to the Brussels riot, his apartment burning, and all of his struggles to survive since losing nearly everything. James' journal was in his home before it was blown up.

The civilians were all chanting about one thing: justice.

Between the massacre that occurred well over a week ago, the people responsible not being revealed, and quite literally nothing being done to mitigate the bombings before the massacre, people had every right to be furious about the injustice against the terrorists or their state. Messland was going to be at war, whether with another country or with its own citizens. It was most definitely a possibility. One that could happen at any time, without warning. There was only one thing people could do: prepare.

James looked around the street and saw that the doors to Cherilym Offices were slightly opened. He knew that nobody had been inside the building since the massacre. He knew that the doors were supposed to be closed off completely. The building was being used by an unknown individual or a group of unknown individuals.

He stepped out from the alleyway and glanced up at the top of the building. At the top of the building, two figures could be seen. James could not make out these figures, but he had a general idea of what they were about to do, based on what was in their hands.

SHATTERED

One of the figures dropped a large and bulky-looking object from the roof before promptly retreating. The other figure stepped back from the edge of the Cherilym Offices' building. Now, they were both out of sight.

James had made out that the dropped object was a bomb. He wasted no time whatsoever to shout "BOMB!" toward the protesting civilians, hoping to get their attention to the new issue at hand.

The bomb had fallen nearly three-quarters of the height of Cherilym Offices, nearing the rioters. James knew there wasn't much time until it would detonate and explode. He didn't waste any more time and jumped back into the alleyway. Not long after, a very loud bang could be heard from the street. The bomb had already exploded.

The following morning, James woke up in a dazed and confused state. He stepped out from the alleyway and glanced around. In an instant, char and ash filled his lungs. The weary man coughed violently in response to the ash and char while trying to see what remained of the rioters, if anything at all.

On the main street of Cherilym, corpses and blood painted the streets. Limbs covered in blood and streets covered with gore. The sight looked right out of a slasher film. Dust filled the air like a snowstorm. The windows of Cherilym Offices were shattered, and the front of the building looked like a bulldozer had rammed into it at full force.

James could not believe what he was seeing. He tried to get up but felt a stinging on his burn. The same burn he got in the previous bombings to the current event. He took a peek at his arm and saw that the wound appeared to have flared up again. Blood came through each individual scar. He knew instantly that the road to recovery would be a long road. While he'd love a good, peaceful life, all good things had to end at some point.

PLAN OF ACTION

"Thank you all for coming," Captain Yuri said. He glanced around the room, meeting the eyes of Daichi, Akio, Kenji, and Aki. "We're here to discuss the bombing that happened in front of Cherilym Offices just an hour ago."

Daichi and Kenji exchanged looks and then glanced back at Yuri. Jackson was standing behind the laptop at the lectern. Yuri gave him a nod, and Jackson tapped the spacebar key. The projector screen changed to blurry and low-quality drone footage. It looked like the footage was from a drone flying overhead the shattered business.

"This footage was captured from a surveillance drone the JSDF has in Messland airspace," spoke Yuri.

Jackson pressed the spacebar key on the laptop, and a video played. The drone was staying in a consistent position high above the granite structure. Two figures could be seen on the rooftop. One of the figures was wearing fully black and with red accents. The other figure was wearing a green ghillie suit.

"These people have been identified to have been the same men who shot up Cherilym Offices not too long ago," the captain declared.

The footage kept playing. The green figure was depicted getting closer to the edge, holding a clunky-looking object with a noticeable glowing red LED light. In front of Cherilym Offices was a crowd, presumably protesting. That was what it looked like in the footage after all. That claim wouldn't be too hard to believe, as the moving pixelated image did look a bit aggressive.

As the footage extract kept playing, the chunky object looked to be dropped onto the crowd, followed by a large, bright orange glow. An explosion. When the explosion appeared to have settled, the road looked to be covered in red, with a small crater where the object struck.

Jackson pressed the spacebar key again, and the video turned to static. The projector screen travelled back up.

"What we have witnessed just now is another deliberate attack on Messland," Yuri spoke with an intense gaze.

Instantly, the room erupted into a discussion frenzy. In the midst of it all, Jackson slammed his fist on the table. The soldiers fell into silence.

After some uncomfortable silence, Kenji raised his hand. "I'd like to object and say that this isn't good news."

Everyone turned their direction to Kenji. He pulled out a laptop and showed images of the terrorist duo. The exact people they were looking for.

"These men are Greene and Crimson," Kenji said, following up on his previous statement. He let everyone have a good look at the image. "Notorious terrorists from Slavic countries. If these sources are correct, they appear to be from Belarus," he said.

"Confirmed, Kenji," Yuri said with a firm expression. "We need a plan of action if we're going to do anything about these two."

The other soldiers nodded along. Jackson took his laptop off the lectern and sat next to his captain at the head of the discussion table. He opened a Word document with the goal of creating a plan of action.

"Ok, we're going to deploy surveillance drones all over Messland," spoke Yuri, followed by the tapping of the laptop keyboard Jackson was using. "We're not allowed to send any drones into neighbouring countries. We're not authorised to." Jackson nodded along as he typed away into the Word document.

"We have about three of these drones with high-quality cameras. These drones will be sent flying overhead in more populated areas. This includes Cherilym, Appletoune, and the villages around the Messland Alps."

Jackson typed up everything Yuri spoke in short, summarised notes. Daichi, Kenji, Aki and Akio nodded along as they took all of this information in.

"Any objections to this plan of action?" asked Yuri as he glanced around the room. No hands were raised, and nobody was indicating they had anything to say. No editorial changes to the plan.

"Very well, this meeting is dismissed," he said. Not too long after, everybody got up and left the discussion room.

COUNTERATTACK

Doomo approached both Crimson and Greene. "Bad news," he said. "They're onto us."

"Who?" asked Greene.

"The JSDF," he responded. "We must lure them to their death."

"How?" questioned Crimson. "It's just the three of us."

"That's what we're going to have to figure out, you red idiot," said the marine. "Consider this, our counterattack."

Crimson interrupted. "How are we supposed to counter a military squad?"

Doomo glanced over at his red comrade. "Leave that to me."

The terrorist in red decided not to question the marine any further. Greene looked at Doomo with scepticism.

"Ok…" he murmured. "But don't do something stupid. One fuck up will ruin this mission."

Doomo gave him a sharp look. "You mistake me for a fool, don't you, shrimp?" he spoke in a condescending and threatening tone. He then approached Greene and punched him in the arm with considerable force. "If you ever say something so stupid again, I will personally ensure your parents are buried next to Stalin's body."

Greene hesitated, then shut up. He took a second to calm down.

"All right, you two. Leave me to figure this plan out," he said. "Now, fuck off right into the forest."

Crimson used this as an excuse to leave Doomo – for whatever reason, he had the terrorist duo meet him in the middle of the forest, not far from one of the villages around the Messland Alps.

The trees in the forest were thick, and the scent in the air was hard to make out, but it was clean air. Fresh air. A rarity.

As Crimson and Greene paced in the forest, Greene checked the time by looking towards the sun – not directly at the sun – and saw the sun setting over the mountain ranges. From what he could tell, the time was around 5:00 pm and 6:00 pm.

"It's 5-6 pm," Greene stated.

"I didn't know you could know the time by looking at the

sun," Crimson observed.

"Comes in handy," Green responded.

"Touché."

PROJECT AMBUSH

Doomo sat at his desk in the hidden facility he constructed.

This facility was built from bricks made from dried mud. The floor of the small facility was made from twigs and leaves. The roof was constructed using dried logs, held up by the strong mud brick walls. This facility contained a single hallway and two rooms. One of the rooms was a storage room, and the other was an office. The facility was lit up by a few lanterns.

Doomo grabbed a pen and a map of Messland. He circled Cherilym, Appletoune, Wellingborough (the major Alps village), a few random houses in the fields, and the Temple of Doom. The Temple of Doom was the same temple he landed in front of a few weeks ago. He picked up some paper from the side and began to write on it.

Project Ambush:

He thought of a strategy to ambush the JSDF squad currently grounded in Messland. After a few minutes, an idea formed in Doomo's head. He wasted no time writing this down before his mind returned to a blank state.

To ambush the JSDF squadron, a method of luring the squad to a random village house needs to happen. Then, a note telling the JSDF to enter the temple should be left in an open and visible location. There's a rumour that, apparently, there's a golem in the heart of the temple. If that's true, we lure the JSDF squadron to go inside the heart of the temple, and then the golem can take them out. After that, we can finally unleash a full-scale invasion against Messland.

The marine read over his swiftly-written notes, mouthing what he'd written to himself. After deciding he was satisfied with the project, he grabbed a stapler and stapled the handwritten note to the map of Messland.

With that, Doomo picked up his work, stepped over to the storage room of the poorly constructed facility, put the map of Messland and the note in his secret vault, and locked the vault.

He stepped back into his office and stepped to the communications desk – the office was set up to have a few different desks for a few different purposes, with one desk being for notes and work (where he was earlier), another desk being for communications (such as radios and communication devices, hence the name), and for leisure.

Doomo turned on his main transmitter and grabbed the microphone attached to the big-looking transmitter.

"Skips, do you copy?" he spoke into the microphone.

"I copy, over," said the pilot. His voice cackled the transmitter's speakers to life.

"A squadron from the JSDF has landed in Messland. They're probably on to us. I have an ambush plan," said the marine, his voice filling Skips' radio speaker.

"Say it, over," responded Skips.

"So…"

Doomo explained his plan entirely, the plan being the attempt to ambush the JSDF and therefore have Messland fall.

"Copy that, over," said Skips. "Requesting permission to inform Greene and Crimson."

"Granted, over," spoke Doomo, then switched off the communication machine.

Doomo blew some dust off the machine's label. The label read 'Eurommunicator,' with the words 'Europe' and 'communicator' being combined. The dust gently floated off the machine and onto the floor, doomed to be forgotten about. The worthless dust, to be forgotten.

Project Ambush:

To ambush the JSDF squadron, a method of luring the squad to a random village house needs to happen. Then, a note telling the JSDF to enter the temple should be left in an open and visible location. There's a rumour that, apparently, there's a golem in the heart of the temple. If that's true, we lure the JSDF squadron to go inside the heart of the temple, and then the golem can take them out. After that, we can finally unleash a full-scale invasion against Messland.

<u>Doomo</u>

DETECTED

Captain Yuri browsed the monitor the drone's cameras were connected to. The monitor displayed what the drone's cameras saw, divided into a few different tables, similar to a security camera monitor. The goal of his browsing was to find any leads on where Crimson and Greene could've been, as well as any potential affiliates of the terrorist duo sweeping through Cherilym.

As proposed, each of the security drones were dispatched to the correct locations, all of which were over Messland airspace.

The captain sat back in his office chair, watching the cameras. In one hand, he was holding a coffee mug. His other hand was over the keyboard of the computer.

As if to answer, one of the drones dispatched over the forest space showed a suspicious figure coming out of the darker part of the forest, lit up only by very few rays of the sun.

Yuri zoomed in on the suspect. The target was wearing a standard Russian marine outfit, with a ski mask over his face. He pressed the spacebar key to take a picture of what the camera saw. Additionally, he took a few more screenshots of the man for good measure, from different angles. The captain had detected a potential target. Just to be safe, he kept monitoring the drone footage, just in case this instance was a false alarm. Safety first, after all.

The time was 4:05 pm. Yuri had been monitoring this one man all day. As the day approached its end, he was growing more and more convinced the man he detected really was affiliated with Crimson and Greene, and not just a nobody.

Yuri glanced up at the clock. It was past midnight, and yet he went to make more coffee. As the coffee was made, he was glancing between the coffee machine and the security monitor, just as if his suspicions would be confirmed, just like that. In all honesty, he could've just opened a screen recording software and rewatched the footage later. However, it was too late, and he was too tired to realise it at first.

He finished making his coffee and returned to his desk. The monitor showed the man seemingly discussing something between Crimson and Greene. Yuri was quick to take a few screenshots of this zoomed-in conversation from different angles. He swiftly copied the screenshots to a USB and placed the screenshots in a Word document. The screenshots were printed on A4 pieces of paper, and the pictures were slipped into one of the desk's drawers. He locked the drawer and finished his coffee.

When he finished the coffee, he switched off the computer and finished work for the day.

DISCUSSION

The following morning, Yuri called in a squadron meeting to discuss his findings from last night.

Jackson was the first to arrive in the meeting room, followed by Aki, Akio, and Kenji. Daichi was absent.

"Thank you all for coming," spoke the captain as he stood at the head of the table. Jackson stood up and approached the laptop on the lectern. He took his place behind the lectern.

"I've made a certain discovery last night involving Crimson and Greene's affiliates."

When Yuri finished speaking, he threw the USB at Jackson. He caught the USB stick and stuck it into the laptop.

"Jackson, could you open the screenshots folder?" asked Yuri.

He nodded, stuck the USB into the computer and opened the screenshots folder. The projector screen rolled down, and it revealed a picture of Crimson, Greene, and a yet-to-be-identified affiliate, all seemingly discussing something in a field, near an old-looking farm cottage. Jackson swiped right and showed another picture, the angle being different but the image being the same.

"We don't know much about this man, but I have reason to believe he's a third member of this terrorist group," spoke the captain in a calm and kind of soothing tone. "Hell, he might not even be a member. He could be a leader for all we know."

Akio and Kenji exchanged confused looks, then looked back at Yuri.

"But, judging by their body language…" Yuri spoke as the picture behind him switched to a close-up shot of Crimson, Greene, and the other man. "… I'm convinced that this third figure is working directly, or indirectly, with the terrorists."

Akio and Kenji exchanged looks once more. Aki nodded along.

"For now, this meeting is dismissed," said Captain Yuri. The captain's tone was laced with authority and command.

Jackson went to leave the meeting room when he was called behind by his captain.

"Hey Jackson, could you stay behind?" asked Yuri.

"Oh, yeah, sure," Jackson responded then stepped toward Yuri.

Everyone else left the room, leaving the two alone.

FIELDS AND WINDS

Yuri took the driver's seat, and Jackson sat in the back seat, rifle in hand. They were on their way to a house in the fields, not too far from a river.

The day previously, he held Jackson behind to discuss something. Specifically, the captain asked the sniper if he could help with a special mission he formed up, dubbed as *Project: Countered*. This was a huge honour to Jackson, being asked personally by his captain and best friend to partake in this mission. Of course, he accepted.

Jackson had his rifle cocked and loaded, his full focus on neutralizing any potential threat. Yuri kept driving the 4x4 scout jeep through the deep forest, navigating the gravel roads.

Eventually, they made it through the forest and into the open fields. The jeep, being a 4x4, made it easier to go off-road. Before too long, the target house was in view. Jackson stood up and spotted a bridge.

The bridge appeared to be made from cobblestone, with wooden fencing acting as a barrier to mitigate accidentally falling off the bridge. The bridge looked kind of old, but it looked sturdy enough to last another few lifetimes without collapsing. It also looked fairly narrow, so a lot of positioning and calculating would be necessary to avoid falling into the river below it or crashing the car on the edges.

"Captain Yuri Katō," spoke Jackson in a firm but clear tone of voice. "There's a bridge to your right. Prepare to direct."

Yuri nodded as he spotted the bridge. "Thanks for the tip, Jackson," he said.

Taking Jackson's advice, he positioned the vehicle to drive safely onto the bridge.

The bridge was crossed, and they eventually arrived in front of the target house. He parked in front of the house and got out of the jeep. The winds have picked up considerably, and the grass danced through the wind with a lot more force than before.

"Ok, which of us shall lead?" Yuri asked.

"I don't know," Jackson responded. "But you *are* the

captain, right?" he proposed.

"You have a point," Yuri spoke calmly, agreeing with Jackson. "All right, I'll go in first."

Yuri held his MP7 submachine gun in his hand with a firm grasp and loaded a fresh round of ammunition. The main goal was to find any intelligence whatsoever. Additionally, the side goal was to counter an ambush in this house, assuming one was set up.

The moment he went inside the house, he was hit with just how stiff and dead the air inside was. The air was so stiff, it felt like it was going to be hard to breathe. This wasn't the case – it wasn't that hard to breathe in, but it genuinely felt like it would be. The house did look really old, to be fair, and not many people would live in a random house in the middle of nowhere. Maybe this was once an old farmhouse? Outside, the wind picked up.

He examined the hallway. Two doors to the left, one door near the front entrance, another door at the end of the hall, and a stairwell right across from the far door. Inside the house, the atmosphere was dead. Like it hadn't been touched in years. The wind outside continued to howl.

Without dropping his guard, the captain turned to the closest door. He proceeded to slowly and carefully open the door. Remaining silent would be impossible as the floorboards creaked beneath their feet and the door hinges creaked loudly. You could possibly hear the hinges outside. Jackson followed him inside as they both slowly crept into the room closest to the front entrance. He gripped the door handle and steadily opened the door.

Jackson watched as the captain opened the door, not knowing what the room might bring. Though the room looked small, a proximity bomb might be placed inside. If that were really the case, *Project: Countered* would be over before it could truly begin.

The brave captain strolled through the doorway and found himself in the kitchen. No bombs, at least. The window, which was tinted from the outside, was massive. It overlooked the valley and into the forest, providing a decent view. It even made up a good part of the kitchen's roof, broken into thirds by the walls and supports.

Yuri glanced around the kitchen entirely and spotted a piece of paper, stuck to the wall and above the stove. It was stuck with sticky tape. With curiosity on his mind, he slowly took steps towards the note. When he was close enough, he read it.

Along the temple,

Lies four of great evil,

Defeat the four of great evil,

Serve thy squadron well.

Immediately, Yuri was suspicious of what the note said. Following through with the note and heading to the temple was just asking to be ambushed and killed on sight. But that did not stop him. If anything, he saw this as a chance to hold the terrorists accountable for their actions and crimes against the innocent civilians of Messland. He yanked the note off the wall and turned around to see Jackson by the doorway, his rifle holstered over his back.

"I found some intelligence in this kitchen," he said and handed the note to Jackson.

Jackson read over the note and raised an eyebrow. "With all due respect, going there would be like holding up a sign that said, 'Please kill me.' We shouldn't go to the temple," he suggested.

"Look, I know this is risky," Yuri responded, "but this might be the only chance we get to make these good-for-nothing terrorists pay." He was asking in a noticeably desperate tone, as if he was itching to hold Crimson, Greene, and possibly the third guy accountable for their actions, while also wanting to do the world proud.

"This is not a good option, yes, but this might be the only one we get," the captain spoke with increased urgency. "Messland is at risk of being invaded on a full-nation scale at any time right now, and we need to stop the threat at its source. The source being Belarus and the borders."

Jackson listened along as Yuri continued.

"So, please, Jackson. We need to get the others on patrol. We have drones to look out for these terrorists. This is *the* best shot we have at protecting Messland," the captain explained, while emphasising that this was the best chance they might ever get, for a while.

Jackson took some time to think before deciding.

"Ok," spoke Jackson, convinced. "I suppose we should."

Yuri gave Jackson a hug of relief. "I promise, this will not go unpaid. I will make sure you get a medal of honour for this and access to anything you need."

The two exchanged this hug for a few more minutes before letting go.

"All right, well, we need to go," spoke Yuri as he returned to his calm demeanour once more. "We need to prepare to storm this temple. We're leaving at 5:42 pm tomorrow."

Jackson nodded before checking the time on his pocket watch – it was currently 2:12 pm. "Yeah, good call."

Yuri climbed into the driver's seat in the jeep, and Jackson jumped back to the back seats. With not much time to spare, they sped off back to their original location.

THAT ROAD

That road. That rocky, dusty, gravel-filled road.

Driving on the harsh gravel road to the temple, from the forest, from the house in the fields, the uneven surface… that road.

Before heading to the temple, Captain Yuri and Jackson took a detour to the JSDF camp, which was based two kilometres from Appletoune. From there, they received some rope, switch knives, three metal water bottles, and a map of Messland. The map showed a dotted trail from the JSDF base to the temple.

The road to the temple, according to the map, was uneven. The majority of the road was laid out around uneven mountain surfaces and unstable cliff ranges.

Maochi, the commanding officer at Messland's JSDF base, caught up to Yuri and Jackson before they left.

"Before you guys go," Maochi spoke. "It might be a good idea to take one of these…"

She glanced over at the garage doors, and the door furthest to the left opened. In the garage, another jeep was stationed.

"This jeep is built for navigating the harsh mountainous terrain," she explained.

With an impressed expression, Yuri slowly approached the jeep. Before he got any further, he glanced over at Maochi.

"Thank you for everything," he said. Jackson nodded along, silently thanking her.

Parked outside of the large temple, the duo looked over the massive temple and then at each other. It was just as they heard: the foundation the structure was built on top of was made from darkened black bricks, some cracked and showing their age. The entrance to the temple resembled a European cathedral, the main structure made from near-identical black bricks to the structure's foundation, with some of the bricks showing their age as well. Overall, the front structure alone was grand, to put it simply. In front of the temple, had two symmetrically placed pillars, made from black bricks and solid gold. However, the pillars showed their age more than the main temple – the left pillar had collapsed, and the right pillar had severely decayed. Behind the entrance, and extending right, looked to be a big wall of some sort. And behind that looked to be some sort of arena.

The captain and the ally stop scouting the temple and meet back outside the entrance. Both of the men felt the heat of the opening coming right at them.

"It seems a bit hot in there," said Yuri. The sniper huddled closer, agreeing.

They both exchanged glances, nodded at each other in understanding, and then entered the temple. The blazing heat got a lot more intense as they ventured forth. Immediately, two lava fountains could be seen on either end. What were the original architects thinking about adding lava? Never the matter. That was not the focus for this mission. The fountain contents flowed down into small pools, blocked off by a steel barrier. Looking up, the duo saw lava blocked off by heat-resistant glass, the glass was being held up by chains and brick supports. The captain's sniper ally pulled out a thermometer and read the room temperature. The temperature recorded was 92°c.

"Jesus…" whispered Jackson. He showed Yuri the temperature, and his eyes widened for a moment in shock, before returning to the neutral and brave expression the sniper was used to.

"It's good we have the water bottles then," Yuri

responded.

As they ventured further into the temple, the bricks looked to decay even further, likely cracking due to the intense heat and overall age. They turned the corner and laid eyes on something they were not expecting.

The hallway from there looked like an obstacle course, with pillars coming out of a deep lava pool. The bricks surrounding the pool were crimson red as if built to house lava. Of course, there was also lava coming from the ceiling, flowing down into the pool below.

"I'm going to test the pillar strength," Yuri declared,

He aimed his MP7 at one of the pillars and fired a few shots. The pillar didn't crumble. It would, potentially, be safe to jump from pillar to pillar. He closed his eyes, took a deep breath, and with nothing but determination being his fuel, he started to dash towards the pillar.

Jackson watched as the captain made the first leap. He succeeded. The pillar didn't crumble beneath his feet, despite looking very unstable.

"They're safe," Yuri shouted unnecessarily. "And a bit hot. But safe because we're wearing boots."

Jackson wiped some of the sweat that was beading from his curly hair and sighed.

"One of these days, missions like this will kill me," he muttered under his breath. He closed his eyes, lost in deep thought.

Leading with your heart can be a terrifying experience. Jackson knew this. This is what made Yuri so great in his eyes – he always had the confidence, the guts, the willpower, the experience… he was just a good friend to have, let alone a good ally and an excellent captain for the squadron.

For a faint moment, Jackson smiled softly and warmly. Despite conditions in the temple being detrimental and demanding, they felt like he could accomplish this task – even with a few sarcastic remarks.

Jackson let out a sigh, opened his eyes, and saw that Yuri had already made it to the other side. Without a moment to spare, he took the first leap. He landed, but the pillar was loose. It shook a little bit upon his feet, landing on the pillar, indicating it was loose and ready to collapse at any time, despite the earlier declaration of safety.

Standing on the loosened first pillar, he knew he had to act fast. There were only three possibilities: Jackson could either leap back to safety, leap to the second pillar, or accept the overly warm embrace of the lava below. This was a life-or-death moment for him. And time was swiftly running out.

The pillar crumbled a bit, the entire left side of the pillar tilting too far back, causing it to fall into the lava. How was this only happening now? The lava should've melted the pillars a long time ago. Jackson spotted the collapsed pillar edge and leapt toward the second pillar. To his luck, he reached the second pillar successfully. However, the first pillar collapsed just after he leapt. The captain watched on as the pillar disappeared into the boiling lava pool, internally thanking god for his ally not being on the pillar for any longer than he needed to be.

Jackson looked behind him, seeing that the pillar had collapsed, and let out an exaggerated sigh of relief, seeing as he just narrowly avoided death. He promptly completed leaping across to the third and fourth pillars.

He spotted the end of the course in range, Yuri standing by the edge. He was ready to assist his comrade if needed. Without much time to spare, he attempted the leap.

Much to Jackson's misfortune, he blacked out. His life flashed before his eyes, watching himself grow up within a few seconds, not even aware that he had lost consciousness. Everything led up to this moment…

BLACKED OUT

Yuri caught Jackson before disaster struck. The captain grabbed his wrist before he could fall into the boiling lava below. He then dragged the sniper to the safety of the stable ground. A bright light was near them, shining through the door arch just past them. It must be the way out of the temple and into the arena.

A few minutes passed, and his ally woke up on the ground. He poured some water over Jackson's head.

"Oh, thank god," spoke Yuri. He was relieved to see his ally conscious. Jackson was confused. He felt light-headed.

"What happened?" asked Jackson.

"You sort of, just, blacked out," explained Yuri. "My guess is you weren't hydrated, and/or the heat got to you."

Jackson rubbed his eyes and looked around. He then saw where the pillars were. The ones he leapt across earlier.

"Oh, right, those pillars collapsed," said Yuri. "I guess the heat got to them, too."

He let out a sigh and stood up. He picked up one of the water bottles he had earlier and chugged nearly the entire thing.

"So, it *was* dehydration…" Yuri murmurs.

"Yep," said Jackson, confirming what his captain thought. Yuri placed the supply bag just by the door arch that led to the arena. They both gave a nod to each other and walked inside.

"Thanks for that," the sniper said, relieved.

"Anytime," responded the captain.

Project: Countered could've been over already if it weren't for Captain Yuri's quick thinking. *Project: Countered* was a short manifesto formed by the chief of the JSDF, given to the captain.

Yuri kneeled down, pulled out the short ten-page document from his vest, and held it carefully. He silently read over the Project: Countered title page in his head.

"I won't let you down, chief…" he whispered to himself.

He thought back to the time when he was with Chief Okoura in the hospital. Okoura was battling cancer at the time, and he wanted to see Yuri on his final day.

"Captain Yuri," he said very weakly.

"Chief," responded Yuri.

He gripped his chief's hand tight. Yuri wanted to help his dying boss in any way. The heart rate monitors were beeping at a slow, but steady rate.

"I want you to have this."

Chief Okoura pulled out a ten-page document and handed it to the captain. On the cover, it read Project: Countered.

"What's this?" asked Yuri.

"It's a draft of a manifesto. We're going to… work to make… Japan a bigger military… power… than places like the United States," explained Okoura, coughing between words in a weak state. "Though… it has your name."

The captain thought to himself for a few seconds. Then, he said, "Why me?"

Okoura coughed a bit more.

"I don't know if it's entirely possible to be a bigger power, so I want… You to decide a new destiny for Project: Countered," the chief explained before breaking into another fit of coughs.

Yuri gripped the chief's hand tighter as he coughed, helpless to this situation.

"Farewell, Yuri Katō …" Chief Okoura whispered weakly

before passing out. The heart rate monitors let out a long beep before falling silent.

The captain let go of the deceased chief's hand. He took off his captain's hat and held it to his chest.

"Thank you for your service," Yuri said before leaving the hospital ward.

Later that night, he reworked the entire manifesto of *Project: Countered.* Instead of the document being about becoming significantly more powerful than the United States, he made it about working to defend weaker nations and supply them with modern military supplies, ammunition, bombs, etc. Places that were unstable, bound to collapse, on the brink of war, invasion, or maybe even both. The captain spent countless hours perfecting his version of *Project: Countered.* Eventually, he finished.

After remembering everything about the document, Yuri took a few seconds before he slipped the document back into his blue captain's uniform. He stood up and turned back to Jackson.

"Are we ready to continue?" asked the sniper.

"Yeah," the captain replied.

TAKING THE BAIT

Captain Yuri and Jackson the Sniper dashed into the arena. It was massive, decayed, and roughly the same size as a two-story gymnasium. Much like the temple it's a part of, the bricks in the arena were decayed and cracked, and even some potholes in the ground had formed.

The duo did not make it far into the arena before they felt the ground shake beneath them. Jackson looked behind him and then tackled Yuri to the side. A large, stone-like golem with red accents all over its body stood in the sniper's original position. If the movement was delayed any further, they'd both be flattened now.

He got off Yuri and pulled him to his feet. An unknown man in a Russian marine's suit and ski mask stood in front of them. He jumped from the back of the golem.

"I see you took the bait," spoke the man in the marine's suit.

"I'm sorry?" questioned the captain. He was confused as to why the Russian man claimed that they 'took the bait.' "Come again?"

"I said you took the…" the golem leapt into the air. "Bait," spoke the marine before the golem fell down toward the brave duo. The sniper pushed Yuri back and leapt to the left before the golem could crush them. Another close call. Dangerously close.

"You guys are very persistent despite being just the two of you," the marine spoke. "I'd imagine there was more of you. I'm Doomo by the way."

"You're one to talk. You hide behind a golem!" shouted Jackson. "You're a coward."

"I'm more than you," replied Doomo. "And you guys will fall alongside Messland."

Yuri knew this marine was serious about his claims. Why wouldn't he be? He'd been hired by the Belarusian government to kill innocent people and even somehow got a golem to do some of the work. If the battle was lost, who knew what the marine would do? Who knew if he was going to send the golem out into the towns and cities of Messland?

The golem leapt up and landed behind Jackson. It prepared a mighty swing. He dropped to the ground, and the golem's stony arm brushed against his soft and curly hair.

"Son of a bitch…" he murmured in a sweat, almost knocked back.

"Too close," Yuri shouted.

Because of how heavy the rocky golem was, its back was exposed for a bit. It wasn't very mobile. Yuri saw that there appeared to be something of a weak point around the centre of its back. The weak point looked like a crystal, and the crystal-like structure was red and a bit cracked.

"I have an idea," he shouted over to Jackson. "Aim for the big crystal on its back, and shoot!"

Doomo watched the golem continue to relentlessly attack both the JSDF captain and the sniper, making slow yet powerful swings. Jackson yanked his rifle off his back and fired a shot at Doomo. He dodged the shot in the nick of time and sprinted away into the temple. The golem turned its attention to the sniper and began to approach him slowly, each step it took causing a shake in the ground.

"Now!" Jackson shouted. "Fire!"

Without much time to spare, Yuri narrowed his eyes, aimed at the target, and fired fourteen consecutive shots at the crystal on the golem's back. Chips of the crystal flew off its back and onto the floor. The golem shrieked in pain and roared in anger. It turned its attention to the captain and began to seek after its attacker. Jackson turned from Doomo's sprinted forfeit and toward the golem. He fired a single bullet at the crystal on the golem's back. A larger piece of the crystal flew off. The golem roared in agony.

Uncontrollably, it started to twitch aggressively. Captain Yuri took note of the twitching. He turned his attention to Jackson.

"Are you seeing this?" he shouted over the angry, painful roars of the golem.

"Yeah," responded Jackson loudly as he reloaded his rifle.

"I'll cause a distraction; you fire the next shot. I think it's on its last leg," shouted Yuri.

"Got it!" confirmed Jackson.

Captain Yuri fired directly at the furthest wall away, opposite the way the duo came from. The golem turned its attention to his position and proceeded to approach him. Jackson aimed directly at the now-glowing crystal on the golem's back, getting ready to fire the last shot. He knew that the glowing was what he should be aiming for – it was coming from the holes the parts from the crystal once held.

"Go to hell," Jackson murmured under his breath.

He fired the next bullet in his rifle. The banging sound rang throughout his ears as the bullet travelled at swift speeds. The metallic lead bullet hit the glowing region in the crystal's exposed point, and the rocky golem roared in pain. It was on its last leg.

The golem fell to its knees, then it fell forward. Its face hit the ground. It was dead. All of the red accents of the golem fell through to the potholes and cracks in the broken brick floor, filling those cracks and holes like a flood.

The brave captain headed to Jackson, and the two met up by the doorway they came from.

"That Doomo guy is still out there," he said, the first to speak.

"And we'll take him out," replied Yuri.

A helicopter can be heard overhead the arena. It slowly descends towards the arena central. When it was directly over, the helicopter descended to both men. Soon after, a rope propelled its way down in front of them. A secondary rope propelled too. Captain Yuri grabbed one rope, and Jackson grabbed the other.

AIRBORNE

As they sat in the helicopter, Yuri looked over the edge of the helicopter. He was lost in deep thought. Jackson looked over at the captain and said nothing for a little bit.

After a while, he decided to break the silence.

"Are you all good?" he asked.

Yuri looked over at him and answered the question. "Yeah, all good. Just tired."

Jackson thought for a bit, then nodded with acceptance. "All right."

The helicopter continued to fly above the valleys of Messland. Captain Yuri looked out the door window of the transport helicopter. He spotted a small farmhouse. It looked to be made of brick and wood, and big enough to contain one bedroom and one bathroom. Across from the farmhouse, not too far away at all, looked like a small wheat and carrot farm, ideal for one person. That property was built in front of a decently sized lake. The water in the lake looked clear, like you could see the bottom of it from a satellite. In between the lake and the wheat and carrot farm was a water tank, and over the farm was a large sprinkler. Taking this into account, the person living there, whoever it may be or would have been in past, would've been very lonely.

"Do you think…" Yuri murmured under his breath. "Maybe, people do bad things, because people just suck?"

Jackson looked over at Yuri and raised an eyebrow, confused. "What are you saying?" he asked.

Yuri realised he had spoken that aloud. He sighed and gave a dismissive hand wave. "Don't worry, I don't know where I was going with that."

Jackson shrugged. "I don't know, you have a point though."

Though he wanted to stop talking, Captain Yuri could not help but elaborate on what he meant.

"Well, some people do bad stuff because of trauma, right?" he asked.

The sniper looked over at his captain and nodded. "True."

Captain Yuri continued. "What about the people who do the bad stuff, just because?"

Jackson raised his eyebrow, then relaxed. "I guess, people are born with bad psychology. Maybe ask a psychologist that question."

The captain nodded in acceptance. "I guess you're right."

September 2024

THE STORM BEFORE THE CALM

The City of Cherilym came into view as the helicopter made it more into the inner district of Messland.

"We'll be arriving soon," spoke the helicopter pilot as the helicopter moved closer and closer. "We'll be landing south of Cherilym."

Jackson looked over in the direction of the pilot. "What gives?" he asked in a confused tone, raising his eyebrow. "Like, not to be rude, but why south of the pinpointed location?"

"You may want to consider the old office building," spoke Captain Yuri as he glanced over at the tower.

Jackson looked over at the building in question. His mouth dropped open and his eyes widened. On the roof of Cherilym Offices was a silhouette of some sort of... dragon?

The helicopter landed in the field just a few hundred metres south of Cherilym. The skies had turned a burning crimson red, and the sunlight had been blocked by the charcoal black clouds. The soldiers leapt out of the helicopter and glanced over at the roof of Cherilym Offices. The duo wasted no time and dashed towards the city gardens, intending to protect the city from further destruction, if it wasn't too late. They raced through the street towards the nature conserve, where they took cover. Yuri stayed behind the doorway, MP7 in hand. Jackson lunged behind a bench in the conservatory to reload his rifle. Captain Yuri peeked out from behind the conservatory's doorway to get a closer look at what was on top of Cherilym Office's roof.

On the roof of Cherilym Offices was a three-headed dragon. Its body structure was created entirely from pure magma and fire. The spikes on its back, neck and tail were made from lava, flowing throughout its body. Presumably, the lava or magma was the blood of its entire being. Its eyes and the inside of its mouth were glowing a bright yellow, giving it a fiery glow. The end of its tail was a magma-like 'U' shape. Its three necks and one tail were long, about the length of a bus or a limousine. Its wings were made of pure fire, supported by a magma structure.

The magma dragon was perched on top of Cherilym Offices like a bird on a tree branch. The captain looked over at Jackson, who'd just finished reloading his rifle entirely and spotted a civilian hiding under a tree. The arm of the civilian was burned horrifically, probably from an explosion a little while ago.

"Civilian sighted!" shouted Yuri. "Do not fire!"

Jackson came out from behind the bench and stood next to Yuri.

"Where?" he yelled, trying to spot the civilian.

"Under that tree!" Captain Katō shouted in response, then pointed directly at the civilian. "We have to get them to safety!"

Jackson nodded, and the duo ran from out of the nature conservancy and towards the stranded man. Yuri hadn't noticed just how bad the city looked – the roads had a few large craters and dents, a ton of the windows in buildings were shattered, and overall, Cherilym was well on its way to looking right out of an apocalyptic film.

Yuri grabbed the uninjured arm of the civilian and dragged him to safety, with Jackson behind them to provide cover, in case of a potential enemy attack. The man didn't try to resist being dragged. He knew it was for his own safety and survival.

Eventually, the captain made it back to the greenhouse and rested the man on a bench, the one Jackson was hiding behind. The toxic smell of smog got a bit worse.

"Thanks," spoke the man weakly. "Yo- you saved my life…" he staggered. "I- I-I'm James…"

"No problem," Yuri said in relief. "It's my jo-"

He was cut off by the loud and intense roar of the dragon. It was being attacked by a tall pitch black, and slim figure, about four metres tall. It had a single magenta eye in the centre of its head, and its jaw was unhinged, revealing sharp black teeth. The tall, slim creature was attacking the dragon relentlessly, seemingly trying to pull one of the heads off the dragon's body. The dragon unleashed a blazing, burning pulse, and the slender figure was sent flying backwards into the road. It hit the road and presumably died. The whole scene reminded Yuri of the Cherilym Office employee who jumped off the building to save his own life, at least that's what he picked up from the clean-up.

It was at this moment that he realised Jackson wasn't with them in the nature conservancy with them. He began to panic, thinking his sniper didn't make it and was still out there, maybe even dead now. Yuri glanced around where they rescued the man. Jackson was nowhere to be seen, and his state of panic got worse. As if his calm deteriorating wasn't bad enough, air raid sirens sounded over him, and a jet engine could be heard flying toward Cherilym. Yuri knew the sound of that specific engine; it was a B-2 bomber. It was from an allied force that thought the city was clear.

Fearing the worst, Yuri urged James to take cover somewhere. James nodded and sluggishly ducked behind the bench. He sighed in approval and sprinted out of the nature conservancy to find Jackson. Before he could get far, he noticed a cylinder-like object falling from the sky. Upon looking at it properly, Yuri knew it was a ballistic missile. It looked powerful enough to take Cherilym off the map. He dashed back inside the nature reserve for cover. He watched as the missile fell all the way to the ground.

When the bomb hit the road in front of the office building, it exploded.

NO WAY OUT

Yuri's ears rang as he slowly came to his senses. He glanced around and saw Cherilym had been bombed. Yuri stood up and saw Crimson and Greene, next to the marine. Doomo was lying on top of the debris that was once the tavern. The dragon's corpse lay over the debris of the office building. The lava was now just dried magma. The skies had turned orange, and the clouds were now a mix of lime and grey.

The two terrorists were at Doomo's side, by the rubble of the tavern. They were trying to get their marine friend to talk, move, or do anything. He let go of Crimson's hand and went into a limp state. The terrorist in the ghillie suit (Greene) muttered a profanity under his breath as he saw Doomo fall.

Yuri pulled out a few combat knives. "I won't go down without taking them down," he muttered under his breath, all while feeling the toxins slowly start to spread through his body.

He aimed one of the combat knives at Crimson and threw it. The blade tore through his back and went right through to his chest. He fell to his knees and collapsed onto the ground.

Greene saw his red comrade fall and charged at Yuri, despite being at a major disadvantage. The captain threw the second knife, but he dodged it in the nick of time. The knife penetrated the dirt.

"You missed, dumbass," Greene remarked in a cocky tone, taunting the captain. He decided to flip him off just for the sake of taunting him further.

Yuri took out a match and lit it.

"You talk too much," he said with a lot of hate. Driven with anger, the match was thrown, and Greene was engulfed in flames before he could react.

As Greene remained in flames, he retreated away from the captain.

"Ohh, fuck," Yuri cursed. "Where's Jackson?"

He tried to stand up, wishing to try and find Jackson, but found his leg was trapped under the rubble. He had no way out. The toxins progressively crept through his organs. Eventually, he passed out, falling back into the debris of the nature conserve. The flames danced around the destroyed buildings, lighting up the evening sky, and sizzling away at the debris.

RESCUE MISSION

Earlier in the morning, a sandstorm came through Cherilym, covering the grass and the destruction and the fire in the sand. Yuri was still unconscious, Crimson was still covered in blood and likely to bleed out, Greene's status was unknown, Doomo was also still unconscious, Jackson's whereabouts were unknown, and there were likely a lot of missing or deceased citizens.

The first week went by. Some sand from the debris had blown away, but the sand that covered the ground was all still there. Somehow, the fires were still all ablaze and probably would be for a long, long time. Not a lot happened in the first week. The second week went by, it was similar to how week one went.

The explosion in the city, which resulted in its total destruction, made global news. With the capital city of Messland in ruins, the leader of the JSDF's specialised rescue team, named Khal, called in the other members of the special rescue squad to have a meeting.

Khal is a young Japanese soldier, around 23 or 24. He had no facial hair, a slight tan, short, messy black hair and deep brown eyes. His voice was deep and smooth, and how he spoke was very clear too. He wore a standard JSDF uniform.

He took his seat at the head of the table; five members sat at the left side of the table, and the other five members sat at the right side.

"Alright. Five of our members are in Messland, previously known as Belgium," the rescue squad leader spoke. "Their names are Yuri Katō, Jackson Herehshie, Daichi Remure, Aki Tanaka, and Akio Suzuki."

The ten other members of the specialised rescue team glanced around at each other, then faced the rescue chief again, waiting to hear what he had to say. This was a dire situation, despite how oddly casual he was.

"Yuri, captain of the Outskirts Squad, was reportedly in Cherilym at the time of the explosion. The status of Jackson, Aki, Daichi and Akio are all unknown," he announced. "All of us are going to go find and retrieve them."

That announcement broke the silence between all ten members of the specialised rescue team. They all broke into a discussion about the whereabouts of these men, what could've been happening before they went missing, and how the rescue squadron was going to find them if that was even possible at this time.

The rescue squad leader clapped his hands a few times, and the team was silenced rather quickly.

"Thank you. I packed supplies ahead of time," said Khal. "You all can take one bag each."

"Oh, ok, thanks," said one of the members from the left side.

"You all are dismissed. You all will have a tracker in the backpack, as well as an M18 pistol. There's a marker on Cherilym. That's what the tracker's for," explained the leader as everyone claimed a different backpack. "The marker on the City of Cherilym is magenta."

One of the members, a male with a typical buzzcut, turned on their tracker. He saw the magenta tracker stated to be around 9,400 kilometres away, the distance between the rescue team quarters (a few kilometres out from the west side of Tokyo), and Cherilym. There were also a ton of cyan markers right next to each other, all in the same location – the quarters. The man turned to Khal.

"Hey, so about all these cyan markers in close proximity to each other…" he murmured under his breath.

Khal took notice of this. "Ah, yes, Zack, there are cyan markers so you guys don't lose each other in Messland."

The man, named Zack, nodded. He then slipped his tracker away. "Neat."

"If the enemy is within range, so are you."
--Murphey

READY

Everyone else was ready. Khal walked out of the room, and the ten members followed behind. They all stepped outside to an airfield just outside of their building, where a C-130 Hercules plane was waiting for them to board. The aircraft was a type of plane made for the convenient transport of troops to foreign countries. While the plane was being fuelled, Khal and the other troops boarded the aircraft.

Before much could happen, Khal turned to face everyone. "Alright, guys. This isn't some sightseeing tourist holiday, as nice as that would be. No. This is a rescue mission," he exclaimed in a stern tone, making sure the other team members heard him. Everyone faced him, indicating he didn't go unheard.

"Excellent," said Khal.

He walked into the cockpit of the plane and tapped on

the shoulder of the main pilot. The main pilot turned around to face him. She looked to be in her mid-20s, and her hair was tied back. Her scarlet lipstick was almost blinding to look at, and her deep blue eyes didn't help either.

"We're all set for take-off," Khal said, giving her the all-clear she's been waiting for. She nodded and started up the plane's engine. The leader paced back into the passenger section and took his seat. Everyone's trackers turned off automatically.

"Hey," said Zack, "so why did our trackers just beep twice quickly?" he asked.

Khal looked over at him. "When a plane engine is on, any of the trackers at least thirty metres from active aircraft automatically turn off. It's automatic flight mode," he explained.

Zack nodded in acceptance, then said, "That makes sense."

The seatbelt light turned on. All eleven passengers put on their seatbelts, and the big door behind them closed so they wouldn't fall out.

"I forgot to mention," said Khal, "The backpack you all received also has a built-in reusable parachute."

"How convenient," said one of the members in a sarcastic way. Though his expression wasn't sarcastic. His expression was sort of grateful for the considerate gesture. "No surprises."

The plane started to move on the runway. Not long after, it took off, and they were all airborne now. They were moving further and further up.

As the plane continued its flight, Khal was monitoring his tracker. They had long left Japanese airspace and were flying over the Pacific Ocean. The pilot sent an automated message ahead of time to the United States Traffic Control with the plane's signal name – "JDF_0431" – with a message requesting to fly overhead US airspace. Not long after the message was sent, the pilot received a message back, informing the JDF_0431 that it was good to go.

Flying over the US wasn't anything special. Though flying over nearly five thousand kilometres of land (most of which consisted of small farms and rural towns) was nothing special, so not much was expected anyway.

Eventually, after flying over the United Kingdom and Wales, they reached the Messland shoreline. Cherilym was in sight over the horizon, and the plane began its descent to the fields west of Cherilym.

The plane landed in the fields. Khal was the first one out, along with the ten rescue squadrons. He overlooked the burning city.

"Follow me," Khal spoke as he made his way into the city. The ten other squad members followed behind him. "We're going to find Yuri and the others."

The air was hard to breathe without getting sneezy or coughing up everywhere. It was laced with sand, dust, and fumes, and smelt like burned char from the Triassic period.

"How did sand get here?" asked Juni, one of the female members of the search squad.

"… Must've been a sandstorm," said Khal.

"But how did a sandstorm happen? There's no desert for thousands of kilometres," said Juni.

"Then either it was somehow blown up from Algeria," the rescue squad leader replied, "or this is nuclear sand."

"Well, if it's nuclear sand, then we're royally fucked," Zack chimed in.

Juni then noticed, "You know, it looks like there was once sand everywhere here. Seems like a lot of it is gone now."

Khal chimed in as well. "Ok, guys, let's just focus on what we were here for: rescue the Outskirts Squad."

SAFE

As Khal paced around the sand, he analysed the environment. A water fountain, presumably from the Cherilym gardens, was destroyed. Just like everything else in the city. He observed that an andesite building and a green building, which were right next to each other, were destroyed and on fire. A small-looking shop to the left of the green building, at least that's what would've been there, was destroyed too.

"Well, that's grim…" murmured Khal to nobody in particular.

He continued to look around. He saw what appeared to be a greenhouse, which was also destroyed.

Khal turned to the other ten squad members and spoke up. "All right, go search the debris. Everyone, get into pairs of two, and look around for the captain," he commanded. The ten personnel followed his request and got to work.

The members of the rescue squad got into pairs successfully a little after Khal spoke. Khal nodded in approval and looked toward what would have been the greenhouse.

"I'll have a look through there," he said as he glanced at it.

Carefully, Khal stepped toward the ruined greenhouse. He had low hopes for this place, but he thought that taking this chance would be the best option. As Khal got closer, he saw a piece of deep blue fabric take flight with the wind and fly away. He took out a photograph of Yuri that he had, and saw that the blue fabric that just flew off matched the type of blue in the photograph. With determination, Khal ran on top of the rubble that was once the greenhouse and started to lift all the loose debris, hoping to find the squadron's missing captain. After a bit of effort, digging through the loose wood pieces, Khal saw Yuri unconscious. He also saw a jean leg sticking out and knew it was a civilian's leg, but there was no way the civilian would be alive. The leg of the civilian was twisted and bent, and very bloody. It was also highly mangled and looked a bit crushed, too, presumably from the bombings not too long ago.

"Found him!" Khal called out to the rest of the squadron. Soon after, the other squad members arrived.

"All hands on deck!" yelled out the rescue team leader. All ten other members jumped up and started helping to dig out the captain, with all hopes being that he was alive.

As they were digging the unconscious captain out of the ruins, Juni spoke up. "I saw three bodies around the green building. The one next to the andesite building. One wearing red, one wearing green, and the other in a Marine's outfit," she said with urgency present in her tone.

Khal looked toward Juni and came up with a plan on the spot. "Very well," he spoke. "After we dig Captain Yuri out, we'll find them. All ten of you can go retrieve their bodies while I take Yuri back to the plane. All hands on deck for this operation!" shouted Khal with command laced throughout his tone.

They all finally get Yuri's body out of the ruined greenhouse. With no time to check for any wounds or injuries, Khal slung him over his shoulders and started to carry Yuri back to the plane. As he did that, the ten other members retrieved the ones in red, green, and the Marine's outfit.

Eventually, they all made it back to the plane, and all four missing persons were rescued…

"Wait, hold on," said Khal. "Where's Jackson?" he asked in a bit of a panic.

"Uhhh… shit," said one of the members, remembering they forgot one of the more important members of Yuri's squad.

Another member spoke up. "Should we look for potential drone footage?" they asked.

"Good call," murmured Khal, who had calmed down a bit. "I have access to the surveillance drone cameras, so I can find out what happened to Jackson," said Khal.

Standing around for a while, he decided to check for the vitals Yuri had. He pressed down on Yuri's chest, wrist, and by his jaw near his neck. There was, thankfully, a pulse in his neck, and he still had a heartbeat.

"Thank god…" murmured Khal, his voice barely above a whisper. "Yuri's safe. Not in the best condition, but safe at the very least," he said.

"That's such a relief!" added Juni.

"Yeah, I agree," Zack said.

Mid-November 2026
(Two years later…)

ROAD TO RECOVERY

Captain Yuri woke up in a strange room, made of quartz. Behind him, the rays from the sun shone onto his face, piercing through the blue window curtains. The floor was made from European White Beechwood. As he sat up on the bed, a young nurse stepped into the ward.

The young nurse was a little bit on the shorter side, a bit slim, and she had orange hair. Her eyes were brown, and she wore rosy-pink lipstick.

"Where am I?" he asked. His voice was croaky and his throat was dry, like he had nothing to drink and nobody to talk to for a long, long time.

"You're in hospital," she spoke calmly as she stepped next to Yuri's hospital ward bed.

"… well, shit," he whispered softly.

As the captain tried to get up, the nurse yelled, "NO!" He

stopped moving and laid back down. "You need to be treated," she said.

The nurse pulled out a needle and stepped towards Yuri's left. He eyed the nurse as she got closer, making out what appeared to be a needle in his peripheral vision. She lowered the bed Yuri was lying on and knelt to the side.

"How long have I been out for?" the captain asked, his voice hardly above a hoarse whisper.

The nurse sighed. "Call me crazy, but you've been out for two years and two months."

Yuri felt his heart start to race in his chest. "What?" he asked. Clearly, he was surprised and even a bit amazed. Two years?

"Tell me about it," she said as she injected the needle into Yuri's left arm, making him flinch.

"Shit…" Yuri softly spoke as the contents of the needle travelled into his arm.

After the needle was depleted, the nurse applied a small needle band-aid over the needle injection site.

"What's your name, anyway?" asked Yuri softly.

"My name is Isabelle," she said. "I'm the nurse who saved you all. I'm also a Messland citizen. During the original attacks from the terrorists, I had to flee to the countryside and get a job here," she explained, her expression hard to read.

"That's a lot to take in, miss," he spoke calmly, feeling guilty about Isabelle's perspective.

"Yeah," she said in a more sombre tone.

"But wait, us all…" Yuri brought up. "Who's *us?*" he asked.

The nurse chuckled, then stepped towards the blue curtain. She pulled it back and revealed a ward to the left of the room that Yuri was in. Crimson was lying on one bed, and Greene was on the other. Doomo was sitting on a chair against the wall, looking mostly recovered.

"Oh, no fucking way…" the captain murmured.

He felt his heart rate speed up upon seeing the three in person, in the same hospital, on the same floor, and right next to each other. He then remembered the past. After the bombings of Cherilym City, he stabbed Crimson and set Greene on fire. Though Doomo was already unconscious. He looked over at the nurse with a confused expression.

Isabelle raised a curious eyebrow and stepped to the side of Yuri. "Do you know these people?" she asked.

Yuri glanced over at her. "No… no, I don't," he lied. She shrugged and left the ward. The nurse left and walked through the corridor and into the elevator. The elevator doors closed, leaving him alone with Crimson, Greene, and Doomo.

The squad captain knew the road to recovery would be hell, but what's important is that he survived the bombing.

He then remembered that Jackson was still missing. However, there was no doubt in his mind that he was alive, somewhere, somehow.

Lost in a trance, he continued to think to himself. He slowly glanced over at the chair by his bed and saw Doomo sitting on it, completely without warning. He jumped at the sight of Doomo, his heart racing faster than before. After a few seconds, Yuri came to his senses and calmed down.

"How was the two-year nap?" asked Doomo. It was clear from his tone that he was just trying to get a reaction from Yuri.

"I'm going to leave now," said Yuri in response.

He stood up from his bed and slowly paced towards the elevator. A weird feeling was brewing in Yuri's gut. He felt like he was in danger just by going near the elevator. This odd feeling didn't stop Yuri as he finally stood in front of the elevator, with the impression that he was just paranoid. The captain clicked the button with the arrow pointing down (the only button) and began the wait. Behind the closed iron door, Yuri heard the sound of the elevator pulley and the noise of the box going up. As this happened, he looked back at the wards every few seconds to make sure one of the three terrorists. or all of them for that matter, were not following him.

After around ten seconds of waiting, the doors finally swung open. Yuri stepped into the elevator. One thing he noticed is that the elevator was somewhat big, and could probably hold twenty people without an issue, not even accounting for removing the railings. The elevator doors closed slowly behind him. Yuri stepped to the button panel and pressed the 1st-floor button. A small jingle started to play as the elevator began to descend. The ward he was assigned was on the fifth floor – the top floor.

The jingle stopped. The elevator stopped going down, too. Yuri prepared himself to step out of the elevator. Whatever was on the other side of the door, he was going to face first-hand. He sighed, and the doors swung open. He was met with what appeared to be some sort of creature.

It was an icy light-blue skeletal structure with no waist or legs – just its arms, spine, ribcage, and skull. Its eye and mouth socket were glowing an even lighter blue. The creature had a void expression, as if its soul was drained from its body. It had a long blue rag going over from its head to its lower spine. That creature also just floated in mid-air.

It leapt out at Yuri, grabbing him and shaking him violently. As it leapt out, the creature let out a high-pitched screech, the screech sounded a bit like a lunar entity.

Jackson traversed through the countryside. He was all on his own, only equipped with a rifle. The weather was overcast outside. The clouds were dark grey. He could smell moisture in the air. Jackson knew it was going to rain soon.

"Fuck, I'm such an idiot…" Jackson murmured as he continued to slowly travel. "I can't believe I left the captain out to die in a fucking missile attack," he said in a raised tone as he continued walking through the empty valley. The guilt of leaving Yuri alone in the city and running off had been eating at Jackson for a long time.

As he travelled, Jackson caught the eye of a tall building, surrounded by a few other much smaller buildings too. He picked up his courage and he started to dash toward what looked like a town of some sort. The closer Jackson got, the more he could see. It was certainly a town, with a hospital just outside.

Eventually, Jackson arrived at the hospital. It was a typical rural hospital, seeing as the town was rural, only having five stories in height. He dashed inside to the lobby to see the windows were completely frosted over and the inside of the lobby was freezing. Strange. It was nearly summer in Messland, right? Why was it so cold? The outside temperature, 19°c, might explain, but overall, it did not make sense to him.

He took out a thermometer from his pocket and held it up toward the air-conditioning unit. The thermometer read a freezing -32°c.

"Holy hell…" Jackson murmured under his breath in a hushed voice. Clearly, something was up. The air-conditioning unit looked to be completely operational and functioning, and there were no weird noises.

"Is this how rural hospitals work?" he asked himself. The hospitals Jackson knew weren't always this cold unless it was the morgue room. The hospital lobby was deserted. Not even the receptionist was present.

Jackson stepped towards the elevator. Strangely enough, it wasn't frozen solid at all, unlike the windows, the lobby seats, and even the wall-mounted TV in the lobby. He pressed the only button to the right of the thick steel elevator doors – the up button. It seemed like the lift wasn't used since the doors swung open. Jackson stepped into the lift and the doors closed. The railings on the elevator were frozen over, and so were the buttons that led to the 1st floor (the floor Jackson was on), the 2nd floor, the 3rd floor, and the 4th floor. The only elevator button that wasn't frozen entirely over was the 5th floor, which appeared to be the highest floor. With hesitation, Jackson tapped the 5th-floor button. The doors closed slowly behind Jackson. He turned to face the doors as they finally closed, and thus, the elevator began its ascension.

After the trip, the doors swung open. Jackson was on the 5th floor. He stepped out and saw the seats outside the elevator were frozen over too. Hesitantly, he took his first step into the corridor and made a right turn. With slowness, Jackson paced through the corridor. His first sight was an open curtain. The ward. It looked vacant. Then he turned the corner and saw the other curtains open. Jackson laid his eyes on Crimson, Greene, and Doomo. Crimson was chugging some alcohol, Greene was flipping a coin, and Doomo was sitting in the seat of the ward across from theirs. The sniper immediately pulled out his rifle and aimed it at Crimson and Greene, in case they were armed. Though it was unlikely. Crimson looked drunk out of his mind, Greene looked confused, and Doomo was just sitting there, unusually relaxed.

"… Well, this is awkward." Doomo was the first to speak.

"Yep," replied Greene, still flipping the coin.

"Oh my god…" said Jackson to himself, as he alternated his aim between the three terrorists.

He stopped alternating his aim at Crimson. "How are you this drunk at…" he checked the time and faced back at the man in the red suit. "At 7:32 am?" he asked.

Greene followed up, not even answering the question. "You know, your friend left a few hours ago. No clue what happened to him, but suddenly it got really cold," he said.

Jackson turned towards Greene. "And why should-"

A screech was heard as the blue skeletal ghost appeared, the same one that caused Yuri's disappearance. The creature turned its attention towards Doomo and held his head with a psychic force.

"Let… go…" stammered Doomo. The creature turned its arm to the right, and Doomo's head fell off. It rolled onto the ground, leaving a bloody trail.

"Holy shit…" murmured Jackson, not expecting this to happen. The creature turned its attention over to Crimson and Greene. Deep blue, icy cylinder-like shapes formed beneath Crimson and Greene, like shadows of some kind. They rose from the flooring below and appeared to completely consume both Crimson and Greene. The irregular cylinder-like shapes descend back into the floor and disappear. The terrorists had gone missing.

The creature turned its attention to Jackson and used a psychic force that blew him to the furthest wall. Jackson flew toward the wall at a fast pace. He hit the wall and fell unconscious soon after. The creature let out another screech before disappearing.

PARANOIA

An iron door slammed shut, and Yuri woke up. He was against a stone brick wall. He looked around and saw he was in a prison cell. Crimson stood over the squad captain.

"Good morning," said Crimson in a snarky tone, trying to get under Yuri's skin, like what Doomo did a while ago.

"What a pleasant way to wake up…" spoke Yuri in a sarcastic response, already irritated.

He sat up and spotted a storage chest in the corner of the cell. Cautiously, he stepped toward it. The captain opened the lid of the storage chest, and Greene leapt out at him. Stumbling back, Yuri fell backwards. He stood back up as Greene stepped out of the chest.

"That was pretty immature," said Yuri, getting over the jump.

Greene snickered at Yuri. "And we're both still here," he said. "All in this cell, going to die from starvation." Clearly, he was not an optimist by any means.

Yuri and Crimson both collectively rolled their eyes at Greene's nihilistic and pessimistic statement. He laughed and approached the cell door.

"Though, I don't know how good this… ghost… is at locking doors…" he murmured. "What if…"

As Greene trailed off, he stepped back to the chest and sat on top of it. The creature appeared outside of the cell bars that separated Yuri, Crimson and Greene from the outside corridor, and glared at them. It let out a high-pitched screech that they were used to as it vanished.

"That… phantom…" spoke Yuri. His voice was hardly above a whisper, like he was trying to comprehend what had happened. "It took me from the hospital."

Crimson and Greene exchanged a look, then faced Yuri with an eyebrow raised.

"When I got out of the elevator, that same phantom leapt out at me, and knocked me unconscious somehow…" Yuri explained.

"Yeah, that ghost thing appeared in front of us," responded Crimson. "It decapitated Doomo and sent us here."

Yuri let out a small whistle in response to what Crimson said. Greene stepped towards the cell door once more. He punched the door, and it fell down.

"Far out…" spoke Yuri, impressed. "I knew ghosts couldn't look through doors, but damn."

Greene beckoned Yuri to follow him. As he started walking towards the man in the ghillie suit, Crimson snuck up on Yuri and punched him in the back of the head. He felt dizzy and fell over. Crimson picked Yuri up by his ankle and dragged him toward the storage chest. Crimson opened the lid and put Yuri in the chest before he slammed it shut.

Once he came back to his senses again, he opened the lid and climbed out of the chest. He groaned, then stepped out of the cell. He looked around the corridor and saw nothing there to fill the silence. Yuri picked up the door Greene knocked over and put it back in place, albeit not to the best it could've been replaced, but he wasn't an engineer by any means. He raced up the stairs to the left of his cell and escaped the prison. Yuri looked back and saw it was a form of underground dungeon.

Paranoia started to fill Yuri's mind as he dashed in the direction of the nearest known Messland JSDF military base. His bearings were always really good, but right now, his bearings were needed more than ever.

Late-November 2026

PHANTOM

"Attention!" shouted a voice over the loudspeakers outside of the gazebo.

Captain Yuri had made it back to a JSDF base after twelve hours of traversing some of the harsh landscapes Messland had to offer. When he arrived, he chugged a whole 350-millilitre bottle of water and rested up. The next day, the captain woke up to the voice over the loudspeaker.

He stood at the head of a meeting table in a Gazebo tent, right next to a JSDF spy. The spy's name was Trent, an American-born spy who worked for the JSDF.

"A meeting will take place in Gazebo Tent G-7. Attendance is mandatory," spoke the voice before the speaker turned off.

Trent stood 172 centimetres. He was rather slim and had a permanent scowl on his face. His eyes were brown, and his hair was dirty blonde. It reached his shoulders. His voice was sharp and commanding. For his spy operations, he wore the type of clothes you'd see someone wear for a night out at a nightclub.

"Thanks for coming," said Trent. "We are all made aware that there's some sort of blue phantom attacking people and armed soldiers alike. It doesn't appear to have a target in mind, but it might spell disaster for all of us."

Yuri felt himself freeze, having come face-to-face with this phantom a few times, having survived the first encounter in the hospital. He chose to remain silent.

"Messland, and Europe as a whole, may cease to exist if this situation goes too far off the rails," said Trent. "We need to take action on this gho-"

One of the soldiers in the middle of the table interrupts, holding up a photograph.

"This is no phantom. It's the Wraith," she spoke. "A deadly frozen creature with no real goal. However, it's extremely hostile, more hostile than that flaming dragon, which died during the ballistic bombing of Cherilym. It's also reported to have more abilities than the dragon, but that's not yet confirmed."

Trent let out a whistle, then started to speak again. "Outside of the gazebo, as you can probably see right now, there is one backpack for each of you."

Yuri looked over at the backpacks just by the *G-7 Gazebo* sign and slowly stepped toward them. Along with a few dozen of the deployed JSDF soldiers currently based in Messland, they all picked up one backpack each.

"When you are done grabbing your backpacks, report back to your seat here," said Trent as he watched everyone collect their backpacks.

After grabbing a backpack, everyone took a seat back at Gazebo G-7. Trent waited for everyone to be fully seated before he started to speak again.

"Alright, everyone, get into groups. We need at least four groups consisting of you lot to have a chance at taking down this Wraith and keeping Messland safe," spoke Trent as he paced left and right of the lectern he stood in front of. Everyone got into their groups of four, all except for Captain Yuri and Jackson, the sniper.

"Jackson and I are going to do this as a duo," said Yuri.

"Well…" trailed off Trent. "You *are* the captain."

Captain Yuri shrugged and then stepped over to Jackson, who was waiting by the G-7 sign.

"We got a city to burn," he said.

The sniper was confused. "… was that a reference?"

Ignoring his question, Yuri pulled out a printed A4 booklet, consisting of five pages. "This is Operation: Frostburn…" he trailed off. "… name still pending."

RESUSCITATION OF CONFLICT

A sandstorm violently kicked up in Cherilym, making sight more difficult than usual. Jackson was shooting his rifle over at an enemy-placed barrier. Behind the barrier stood Crimson and Greene.

On the previous day, Captain Yuri showed Jackson the entire *Project: Frostburn* manifesto. Page one provided a summary of what the plan was about. The second page explained that taking out The Wraith was the main priority. Page three was about taking out the Belarusian terrorists, with the fourth page providing three methods of carrying out the plan. Page five consisted of a map of Messland, with red pen marking key locations (Cherilym, the Alps, bases, the temple, etc).

On command, Jackson fired another shot at the barrier,

the bullet striking the bottom of the concrete.

"Far out… shooting in a sandstorm is harder than it looks…" spoke Jackson. "I just want this war to end," he said.

"I get that," said Yuri. "Getting dragged into a conflict in Europe was definitely not on my bucket list, but y'know, it's what we have to do to save this developing nation. It came back from an all-out collapse, after all. Messland's troop base just isn't equipped t-"

The captain was cut off by rapid fire coming toward them, and he ducked behind the barrier Jackson was hiding behind.

"Taking fire!" he shouted as he reached for his MP7. The submachine gun was placed by Jackson in the sand. Additionally, there were a few grenades there, too, ready to be thrown.

"Just take it!" shouted Jackson as he nudged the weapon toward Yuri with his foot. The captain picked up the MP7 submachine gun and peeked over the concrete barrier. Yuri then ducked back behind the barrier and picked up a grenade. The sandstorm had started to subside a bit, but it was still raging on. The subsiding revealed just how orange the skies were and how grey the clouds were. It was a bleak and apocalyptic sight.

Crimson, Greene, and their concrete barrier were a lot more visible. Captain Yuri pulled the pin back and held the grenade behind him like a shot put. He threw the explosive over at Crimson, who was the most exposed. Air raid sirens began to blare out, the noise making the JSDF duo wince. The siren was just ten metres to their right. However, they did not let the sudden loud tones interfere.

He threw the grenade toward Crimson. The bomb flew through the air. Since this was happening, it was clear: this was a resuscitation of conflict – the Wraith, the Belarusian invasion of Messland, and miscellaneous tensions all over the world.

"Get down!" yelled Greene as the grenade landed right next to him. Crimson leapt back behind the concrete barrier, and the grenade exploded. The concrete barrier saved the terrorists' lives.

"Damnit," the captain murmured under his breath as the dust settled, revealing a small sandy crater. It was roughly the same size as a hole you'd dig at the beach to bury yourself for fun.

Jets could be heard flying nearby as the air raid sirens continued to blare. When the jets were right above Yuri and Jackson, a small grey object fell from the jet as it flew into the distance. The object hit the ground, and it exploded into a large veil of dust and smoke.

"Smoke grenade!" yelled Yuri. Both soldiers got down behind their barrier. Footsteps slowly approached; the unknown person's feet trudged through the sand, making soft distinct patting noises.

"Keep your guard up," whispered Yuri. Jackson doesn't

respond immediately. Yuri doesn't think much of the lack of response at first. Maybe he didn't hear?

ONE WAY OUT

"Keep your guard up," whispered Yuri. Jackson didn't respond immediately. Yuri doesn't think much of the lack of response at first. Maybe he didn't hear?

The smoke settled. The captain looked over to see Jackson, against the concrete block. Then, he looked down and saw a pool of blood. In a deep panic, he looked at the sniper's chest and saw a knife in it. He then saw a man in red and grey, looming over him.

Their eyes were red, and his pupils were crimson. They were covered in red with grey accents, sort of like armour. They definitely were not a human. The man looked man-made, like, made in a lab.

Yuri started freaking out. He just watched his best friend and, quite frankly, the one he trusted most, get murdered right in front of him.

"What the hell…" Yuri stammered out. The humanoid

grabbed the knife from Jackson's chest and sliced Jackson's head from his body. His head fell onto the sand, painting it red. The humanoid then chopped off Jackson's right arm and then dropped the knife. Deciding he saw enough, Yuri sprinted away as fast as possible. He ran and ran, MP7 in hand. As he ran, he shot a few blind shots at the humanoid, all of which missed. Since Yuri was in a desperate state, all the shots he took missed. There was only one way out. Retreating.

STRESS RESPONSE

"I'm so fucking stupid…" murmured Yuri as he slumped against the wall of his office, which was not too far from Appletoune City at all. "Why did I only bring Jackson with me? Why didn't I get a bigger group?" he asked himself.

It had been a few days since he watched Jackson get killed in front of him. The image hadn't left his mind at all. His mindset deteriorated considerably, despite it only being a few days since witnessing what he had to witness. Yuri hadn't cried in years. Despite witnessing the one he trusted most get murdered in front of him, he still couldn't get it out. The image of Jackson being mutilated keeps playing back in his head. He was going through a lot of distress. The feeling of this kind of stress response was a feeling Yuri hadn't felt since he was at least fifteen years old. Dark circles spiralled around his eyes like a never-ending void.

Yuri's phone starts ringing. It was Trent. Yuri picks up the phone.

"… hello?" Yuri whispered.

"Hey, it's Trent."

"…"

"I'm sorry about Jackson," said Trent.

"…"

Yuri hung up the phone. He put his phone on 'do not disturb,' then slipped it into his pocket. He stayed slumped against the wall. The hunger he felt initially was gone.

Mid-December 2026

RESURGENCE

Yuri woke up in a cold sweat in his apartment around the Messland-Germany border. Not a surprise. He clicked on his phone and saw the time was 4:12 am.

Overnight, he had a nightmare. He was in a dark, frosty cave, shivering. There was no way out of the cavern. He looked around and saw the Wraith and Jackson's corpse hanging from a rope, which was attached to an ice spike on the ceiling.

It was at this time that the grieving captain decided that right now would be a good time to start the day. Every day is a new day. The scars of the previous day still show on the new days.

He had a shower, drank some coffee, watched the morning news, drank some more coffee, changed from his white singlet and black long pants into his signature blue captain uniform, slapped on his black military captain hat, and then stepped onto the balcony. Yuri had started to feel sick at the thought of the day, December 17th, the same day he returned to military service, but that was how it was meant to be. This day was Yuri's resurgence, no matter what.

He left his apartment building, got into his Toyota Yaris, and drove off to the main Messland military base, located a few hundred metres south of Appletoune.

NOT BACKING AWAY

Yuri parked his vehicle in the parking lot of the facility. He had no clue what to expect for the following days, months, or even years. However, one thing was clear: he was a captain. Captain Yuri Katō was not backing away. MP7 in hand and bags under his eyes, he continued to pace into the JSDF Messland base. As nervous as he was, Yuri was not backing away. He can't. It'd be a waste.

"All right, guys." A female voice could be heard at the head of the table. Captain Yuri entered the briefing room and sat in the middle-right seat. "I'm Commander Riley. I was asked to take over for a bit."

He looked over at Riley, the acting commander. The commander role was much different from the captain role that he occupied – commanders kept the operations running smoothly. She had deep brown hair with streaks of deep green dyed into it, magenta pupils (likely contacts), and a rose pin on her uniform. She also deep purple button-up shirt and long black jeans with black leather shoes.

"When I call your name, come on up and collect a backpack kit," she explained as she eyed everyone in the room. Her tone of voice was sharp and authoritative, but genuine too. "The kit will have everything you need for that specific mission."

Yuri sighed. First day back after watching his best friend get mutilated, and already off to a mission. This was a military job, so he sort of expected it, but even so, he knew he was in for a long ride.

"Captain Yuri," Riley spoke. "Your kit can now be collected."

He got up and stepped to the far right corner of the room, where the kits were. He picked one up and slung it over his shoulders.

"Thanks," he said before he left the room.

When he arrived at an empty room, Yuri kneeled down and unzipped his backpack. He found a few bottles of water, a few blank pieces of A4 paper, two pens, and two premade sandwiches (both sliced into triangles) in a triangle sandwich container. One of the sandwiches was chicken, and the other was ham and cheese.

Yuri zipped up the backpack and left the room with a

blank expression. From the room he was in, it wasn't too far away from the parking lot whatsoever. He trod down the hallway and stepped outside into the parking lot. He got into his Toyota and drove into the town of Appletoune.

After arriving at a parking lot just outside of the town, he parked his car and stepped into the streets of Appletoune. Captain Yuri was informed that Crimson and Greene were around this location, and he wanted to get some form of justice for his fallen friend.

DISASTER BREWING

As he paced down the streets of Appletoune, Yuri heard thunder. It rumbled intensely in the distance as he sprinted through the streets of the much larger Appletoune. This city felt more like a city than what Cherilym once was, and it looked much more European, too.

Despite a storm rolling through, the streets were oddly crowded. There were a lot of people out and about, all chatting with each other like it was a community event. Captain Yuri sprinted past everyone in the crowd, narrowly avoiding hitting a few. It probably wasn't a smart idea to hold his MP7 in his hand while sprinting through public, but the captain didn't care right now. That wasn't his worry.

He arrived at the train station and waited for the next train. It was to a small town right next to the Messland Alps, with two main streets, and the town's name was 'Blackspike Town,' as bizarre a name as it was.

Crimson and Greene were inside one of the buildings in Appletoune, just hanging out and waiting. This was a club from the 1950s that 'closed down.' Greene was holding a walkie-talkie, and Crimson was holding a Glock-18.

"When are we going on our mission?" asked Greene slowly.

"Soon, I'm sure," said Crimson. He seemed uninterested.

The walkie-talkie crackled to life. The output sound was cracking up a lot. "It's time to go," was heard over the static.

"Fucking finally," said Crimson as he jolted to life.

The train had nearly arrived at the station. Its brakes screeched as it came to a complete halt. Yuri boarded the train and sat closest to the middle door, the door he boarded through. He mounted his MP7 onto his belt. It felt oddly light…

The doors on the train closed, and it took off, leaving Appletoune. Yuri knew this was a part of the mission. He could've chosen to drive his way to Blackspike Town, but judging by his current state, the captain decided it'd be best to catch a train instead. In retrospect, he could've gotten a fellow troop to take him to Blackspike; however, he didn't think of that. He was simply too distressed about his work. He was simply too distressed about what he witnessed. The train continued down the tracks as Yuri lost himself in thought.

It didn't take long for the captain to realise he was sitting next to some guy in his early 20s. The guy he had sat next to was wearing a blue cap, facing backwards. He was wearing a grey shirt, long beige pants, and white joggers. He had short, light brown, curly hair, too. Yuri chose to keep quiet. The guy looked over at the military captain, shrugged, and pulled out his phone.

The train continued down the tracks at a relatively fast pace. The tracks went right through the forest that separated both Appletoune City and Blackspike Town. Raindrops could be seen splatting against the windows and the walls, and the roof of the train. It was starting to rain. Thunder could be heard rolling in as well.

The train arrives at Blackspike Town Station. The screeching of the brakes could be heard from even inside the train. When the train stopped at the station, he stood up and stepped onto the platform. Immediately, It was obvious that the rain had gotten much more intense. Yuri looked over at the mountain ranges and saw a lightning bolt strike around the top of one of the larger surrounding mountains.

"This mission is going to be hell..." he murmured to himself. "This mission is a disaster brewing..."

HELD UP

Captain Yuri dashed through the streets of Blackspike Town. The rain had picked up a lot. Thunder continued to growl over the distance.

Yuri made his way through an alleyway and onto the other main street. He stopped and looked around. This street was dead. The previous street had a few people out, but overall, this town was dead. Yuri knew Blackspike Town was rural, and rural towns were typically dead, especially during weather like storms.

Without warning, all the sounds of the people chatting and living their lives in the previous street were quickly replaced with screaming and gunshots. Yuri ducked into the alleyway and held his MP7 tight. When the screaming died down, Yuri glanced over and saw a familiar figure approaching in his direction.

Cautiously, the captain climbed out from the bush he hid

behind and saw Greene stepping his way, holding a loaded Glock-18. Crimson came out from the alleyway, following behind Greene. He was holding an assault rifle, the same one he was holding the entire time.

Yuri aimed his MP7 at Crimson, alternating his aim between the two terrorists. Greene got close and held the Glock-18 at Yuri's head. Yuri tried to shoot a shot at Greene, only for a click to be heard. A faint, silent click. Yuri was out of ammo, and being held up.

"So glad that Android took out that damn sniper," yelled Crimson, sounding delighted.

Yuri gave Crimson a death glare and yelled, "Go to hell!"

Greene laughed at Yuri's insult. "See you *and* your friend there."

Greene's finger wrapped around the trigger of the Glock-18 pistol. He was ready to finally put an end to Yuri.

"Any final words?" asked Greene, malice laced in his tone. Yuri remained silent and threw his weapon to the side. Crimson chuckled.

"Very well…" murmured Greene.

Before Greene could deliver the final blow, a tank could be heard rolling towards them from the forest opening. Additionally, a trap remix of the United States national anthem could be heard blasting from a boombox. Crimson turned around to find the source of the noise, and his eyes widened.

In front of Crimson was a large grey steel tank rolling towards them. It was an M41 Walker Bulldog, one of the tanks from the Cold War. The tank stopped right in front of them. The barrel pointed above them, aiming into the skies above. The hatch in the lid opened, and out came a man in full body armour.

SAVED

The man fired a cannon into the sky. A loud explosion could be heard as the cannon was fired. It made its way from the barrel up into the sky at a rapid pace.

Crimson and Greene's jaws dropped, and both their eyes had widened. They dashed away in retreat, not wanting to be at the receiving end of the barrel. Yuri looked over at the man in armour. He was saved.

The man wore grey armour with organised light blue lighting going across the sides, sort of like cartoon outlining. The grey armour was steel and looked very tough to pierce. The light blue glow was also present around the eye sockets of the helmet, which the helmet took over the man's head. Not a single part of his skin was visible.

"Who are you…" stammered Yuri after taking a few seconds to process what just happened.

"My name? It's Aqua. I'm the co-leader of the United

States Super Soldiers," the man, named Aqua, spoke with confidence. No doubt, he was cool.

"No fucking way…" the helpless captain stammered.

Yuri knew about the Super Soldiers. Their training was more brutal than typical soldier training environments. But the pay-off meant access to the deadliest and most lethal weapons, such as literal laser guns and powerful rail guns. It was almost like the Super Soldiers were pulled right from a science fiction film, but right there in real life.

Aqua held out a hand for Yuri to take. "I'll explain everything later," he said.

Without hesitation, he took Aqua's hand. They both took to the tank. Aqua got into the operations hole he was just in, and Yuri sat on the side of the tank. Aqua left the hatch open as they drove down into the other forest opening.

EXPLANATIONS

The tank rolled through the open valley. Up until that point, Yuri was silent.

"So…" spoke Yuri, then stood up. He gripped the edge of the outer hatch that Aqua was in. "How did you know I was there?"

Aqua let out a hearty laugh. "Oh, that was an accident." His voice sounded a bit muffled and restricted through the helmet, but it was still very clear. "We've been tracking Belarusian terrorism for a while, and we knew terrorists would go for Blackspike Town, just to kill off residents."

"Ok then," said Yuri, not questioning any further.

"By the way, I've also been deployed to help out your JSDF against the Wraith. We Americans fear that the Wraith will come for us next. As the story goes, the Wraith prefers environments with snow," explained Aqua as he kept alternating his sight between Yuri and the road ahead, making sure he didn't go off track and crash into a tree or fall into a ditch.

"So, the Wraith prefers cold environments… and it sees us humans as threats?" asked Yuri.

"Oh yes," said Aqua. "That thing will stop at nothing to make sure it lives in a cold environment alone. Don't be mistaken about it being a plain and simple savage."

Yuri let out a small whistle at what Aqua said.

"I know where a laser weapon is located," said Aqua. Yuri looked over at Aqua. "Basically, I need you to keep a lookout and help me retrieve it safely."

"And… what's in it for me?" asked Yuri.

"Good question," said Aqua in response. "I mean, that uniform you're wearing… you're a captain then?" he asked.

"I- yeah." Yuri was a bit flattered that his captain's uniform was recognised, but didn't let it show. He thought he was coming off as a bit of a nervous wreck.

"Cool, cool," nodded Aqua.

After a few minutes of silence, Yuri had a topic he wanted to answer. He looked over at Aqua.

"By the way," he spoke, "how do you know there's a laser gun around here?" he asked.

"Ohh, that's confidential," Aqua replied.

The journey felt like it had been going on for a few hours now. During the hours-long journey, it seemed like the only conversation happening was mindless small talk.

Eventually, they came across a windmill, but without its blades.

"Jackpot…" said Aqua. He sounded excited. Yuri chose to remain silent.

Aqua pulled the tank next to the windmill and parked it. He pulled out a tracker and turned it on. There was a beeping that sounded like a metal detector.

"Found it," he said.

"Found… what?" asked Yuri

He climbed out of the hatch and onto the grass. Yuri jumped down from the side and landed next to his new ally.

The windmill was in the middle of a valley. The reason why it was built there, let alone built at all, was unknown to either Yuri or Aqua. It was made from wood with brick outlining. The windmill looked old, almost like it was built over one hundred years ago. Maybe it was once a farm?

"Bloody hell, this thing looks like it's one storm away from blowing over and collapsing," said Aqua, sounding a bit amused. Yuri continued to remain silent.

Yuri approached the door to the windmill and opened it. The Super Soldier followed behind closely.

"If I had to guess…" he murmured. "It'd be up the top of that ladder."

Yuri looked inside and saw a ladder leading all the way up that he hadn't even seen originally. He approached the old ladder and saw it led to what appeared to be the top of the windmill.

"Only one way to find out," said Aqua as he stepped in front of Yuri. He climbed up the ladder. The captain didn't question how the ladder didn't just snap under Aqua, let alone while he was in heavy armour. However, it was simply amazing. Yuri climbed up behind him, a bit slower, being careful to avoid the rope and the planks potentially giving way and snapping.

Both soldiers climbed to the top of the windmill and saw a balcony, built into the top that overlooked the distance. A storage chest behind the ladder captured Aqua's interest. He opened it. It was filled with dirt, gravel, and stones of varying sizes. There was also a faint yellow glow beneath it.

"Yuri, was it?" he asked enthusiastically. "Come help me dig all this."

The captain looked over and saw Aqua holding the chest lid open. He stepped over and started digging through the minerals and dirt. The contents inside the chest spilt onto the plank floor and the stones were thrown over the balcony. Gradually, the bright yellow glow got brighter and brighter. Soon enough, they reached the bottom of the chest. Aqua reached in and pulled out a white blaster rifle with bright yellow LED lighting across the sides. It was some sort of energy gun.

"Holy hell…" Aqua said, expressing astonishment.

"What the fuck…" murmured Yuri.

Aqua held the blaster rifle tight. This thing was a rifle with another barrel. It looked capable of firing energy sources as if it were a rail gun, though it clearly was not a rail gun.

"This must be it…" whispered Aqua. "… the gun my instructor told me about."

"Your… instructor?" asked Yuri.

Aqua froze and looked over at Yuri. Then he got more energetic. "Oh, well, no point hiding it now," he said. "My instructor. We Super Soldiers have to go on a mission to find our weapons, rather than just having it handed to us. Personally, I was sent to Messland, where my weapon was, to help fight off the Wraith."

Yuri was confused, but let Aqua talk some more.

"With this, one quest is over, and my next quest is ready: Help the JSDF fight off the Wraith and save the Northern Hemisphere."

It finally made sense. Yuri finally, to an extent, understood what Aqua was on about. His high energy, his explanations about Super Soldier duties on the way there… it all made sense to him.

As the excitement was real, a loud crash could be heard. Yuri looked outside and saw a small fire in a tree. So much had happened within the past day that the fire in the tree didn't shock him.

Aqua looked at Yuri and cleared his throat. "Alright, we got what we wanted, let's leave."

Yuri nodded. Aqua slid down the ladder, and Yuri slid down when Aqua was down. They left the windmill. Aqua climbed into the control hatch of the tank, and Yuri climbed back onto the side.

"Where are we going?" asked Yuri.

Aqua looked over at Yuri. "We're going to the Messland JSDF base, where you guys are based right now."

"… Yeah, good call," said Yuri.

The tank engine started up and left for the direction of the JSDF base, the one located near Appletoune.

INTRODUCTIONS

The M41 tank arrived at the tank depot at the JSDF base. Aqua parked the tank at the closest shed to the boom gate. Yuri leapt from the tank in the shed. The Super Soldier got out of the hatch soon after.

"I'll take you to the briefing room," Yuri offered as he held out his hand towards Aqua for a handshake. The Super Soldier took his hand and gave it a tight shake, holding the blaster rifle in his other hand. The handshake he gave nearly broke the captain's wrist. He caught wind of this and quickly let go, realising Yuri's discomfort.

"Err… sorry," Aqua said.

"It's fine," he said. He shook his hand and cleared his throat.

"Alright, let's go," he said and started to walk towards the depot entrance to the building, expecting Aqua to follow behind. As expected, he followed behind Yuri.

"So, I'm going to introduce you to the JSDF members based in Messland, ok? There are about 200 soldiers based here, so we'll hold an introductory meeting," explained Yuri as he walked. Aqua nodded along. He accepted something like this was going to happen at some point.

Captain Yuri stopped in front of the empty meeting room. It was like a big canteen, without the food. The way the tables were scattered around the room, and the way there was a large lectern at the far end of the room, directly opposite the large opening.

"Ok, this is a big room," said Aqua, a bit stunned.

"Yeah?" said Yuri in response. He was amused at Aqua's observation. "This room can host up to six hundred people, you know."

"Yeah…" Aqua murmured in agreement, still very much astounded. "I got that impression."

Captain Yuri walked toward the lectern at the far end of the table, with Aqua following behind. He stood behind the lectern, and he stood next to the captain. He picked up a landline phone from the lectern top and dialled a number. Yuri held the phone to his right ear, and the overhead facility speakers crackled to life. He spoke into the phone's microphone, his voice projecting over the facility speakers.

"Attention everyone, a mandatory meeting is being held in Depot Block A-0. I repeat: a mandatory meeting is being held in Depot Block A-0."

After he made the announcement, Yuri hung up the phone, and the speaker system silenced. Not long after he spoke of the announcement, the room gradually started to fill up with other Japanese troops based in Messland. Slowly but surely, everyone who was present in the facility was in the large room, sitting at a table.

Aqua turned to Yuri and nudged his side. "That worked as well as you hoped."

He looked down at the Super Soldier and had a small smirk. "Well, it is mandatory, to be honest."

Now, everyone had arrived and had taken their seats. Yuri grabbed the microphone from the lectern in front of him and turned on the speaker system. He flicked some switches, and the microphone was connected to the room's speaker system. He tapped the microphone and started to talk.

"Thank you all for coming today," said Yuri. "I called this meeting to introduce a new temporary co-leader."

Aqua stood up next to Yuri. He held his blaster rifle firmly in his hands.

"This is Aqua. He's one of the few Super Soldiers from the United States. He's been deployed here from North Carolina's Super Soldier academy to help fight one of the biggest lone threats there is, the Wraith."

As he spoke, a screen rolled down and a clear photograph of the Wraith was visible. There it was, in its ghostly skeletal husk. The whole room was left speechless at the horrific sight of the monster.

"The plan stands. You guys, get into groups of four. Ideally, forty people per group or more. Aqua and I will stick together and take on the Wraith head-on." As he explained this, everyone slowly and collectively nodded along with Yuri's speech in agreement.

"Alright, everyone. GO!" shouted Yuri into the mic. "Introductions are over, let's go now. We have ourselves a monster to defeat."

Everyone in the room started to get into their groups as Yuri looked over at Aqua.

"Aqua, come with me. I'm going to arm up," said Yuri, then stepped into the corridor, expecting him to follow behind.

"Yeah, ok, sure," Aqua said before he followed behind.

ARMOURED UP

Captain Yuri and Aqua (the new co-leader) walked down the hallway. It was a pretty long hallway.

"So, where are we going?" Aqua asked.

"Oh, we're going to the armoury. I'm going to need a new MP7," the captain said.

"What happened to your old one?" he asked.

"Oh, I lost it before you rescued me," explained Yuri. "You see, it was out of ammo and I was about to die, so I dropped the weapon. I forgot to grab it before leaving with you on the tank."

"Ahh, that makes sense," Aqua said.

They both arrived at the front of the armoury's large door. Yuri swiped his clearance card, and the large metal door opened. Aqua is met with a large weapons arsenal.

They both step inside to reveal a library of weapons, each divided into different shelves and tables. They were all in their own separate sections – handguns, rifles, automatic weapons, heavy weapons, explosives, and melee. A section with miscellaneous tools was also present, with torches, compasses, etc. Despite being armed with a literal superweapon, Aqua was stunned at this revelation.

"Our budget was increased by a lot from the Japanese Government, meaning we're more than well-equipped to take on the Wraith," explained Yuri as he stepped towards the handgun section. The air inside the armoury was cool, but not quite cold. It was like stepping into a museum, with the walls being made from tile and the floor being covered in smooth, deep red carpet. Pillars also held up the ceiling.

"And it shows," replied Aqua, still taking this in.

Yuri came back out after a few minutes, holding two MP7 submachine guns, one in each hand. He looked over at the captain and let out a small whistle.

"You look badass, not going to lie," said Aqua as he finished processing the armoury.

"You have my permission to take any weapon you want as well," replied Yuri, pointing his left MP7 around the armoury, then back down to his side.

"Don't mind if I do," Aqua said blankly.

And thus, he looked around the armoury. He glanced around at each of the weapons. He already had a rifle – he decided on heading toward the handgun section where Yuri was just at.

"Any chance a handgun can shoot grenades?" he asked as he looked around.

Yuri chuckled, then turned his body around to be face-to-face with the explosives section. "You'll want to have a look through the explosives aisle for a grenade launcher."

Aqua whistled and stepped toward where Yuri said the explosives were. He found his grenade launcher. It was designed to look like a regular pistol.

"This is cool!" Aqua exclaimed, the blaster rifle by his feet as he spun the grenade pistol around his finger.

"Tell me about it," said Yuri.

After a few seconds of Aqua spinning the pistol around his finger, he placed the pistol back where he found it.

"You're not going to take it after all?" asked Yuri.

Aqua shrugged. "Nah, I still got this sweet blaster rifle." He picked it up and pointed it up at the ceiling.

Yuri shrugged and didn't question it. "Ok, then. After this, I have to check up on our spy. They might have some intel on the Wraith…" he murmured. "… don't get your hopes up, nothing's guaranteed."

All armoured up, the two walked out of the armoury, and

they stepped further down the corridor.

"After this, if there's anything at all," said Yuri, then he stopped walking and looked right into the glowing blue eye sockets of Aqua's helmet. "We're going to war against the Wraith."

Yuri continued walking down the corridor and eventually reached the intelligence room. Aqua was right behind him.

"This is where the spy's fax machine will be. She's usually out and about, so sending the information through fax, whether it's a written note or a photograph, would be our best bet," he explained to Aqua as he opened the door with his keycard. Yuri stepped into the room, followed by Aqua. The fax machine was right there. It was printing something.

The intelligence room itself was dimly lit and very small – about the same size as four conjoined office cubicles, but made from roughly the same interior as the armoury.

The printing finished, and a piece of paper was sent into a bin. The fax machine was set up in a way that all printed material was sent into a bin for later collection.

"Perfect," said Aqua.

"Right on queue," replied Yuri.

He put down both MP7 submachine guns on a table and picked up the paper from the bin. He turned on the desk light and held the paper beneath the light. It was a photograph of sorts. It was a cold snowy forest, appearing to be surrounded by massive snowy mountains. Yuri knew this was around the Messland-German-Netherlands border, meaning he and Aqua would have to go pretty far up North-West from their current position. The photograph showed a small castle made from snow and ice. It looked like you could walk right through to the throne room, there being no door.

"This is pretty good," said Yuri as he beckoned Aqua to approach. When he was close enough, Yuri showed him the photograph that was faxed over.

"That's convenient," said Aqua in response. "It's like this damn phantom wants to die."

As the two men shared a laugh, a picture of the Wraith right by the castle entrance was printed. It looked like it was facing the camera itself.

Aqua picked up the image and showed Yuri.

"Well…" murmured Yuri.

A third printing came through the machine. It was the simple phrase '*It got me.*' Yuri felt a cold tingling travel down his spine.

"Holy hell…" murmured Aqua as he read the message.

"Damnit…" Yuri whispered under his breath.

He crumbled up the message and faced Aqua.

"We have to go!" he exclaimed.

Aqua nodded and dashed out of the room towards the

depot, and Yuri followed behind. They sprinted up to the helipad to see a helicopter waiting for them.

"This is it," Aqua spoke.

"Yeah," Yuri agreed.

They climbed into the back of the helicopter. Shortly after, it flew off. The sun was setting, and the two soldiers knew they'd arrive at the site very late at night. The captain looked over and saw that there was a table next to the left door of the helicopter, with a designated coffee station ready.

"Jackpot," Yuri said.

SCALDING CONFLICT

The helicopter had already been flying for a long while now. Yuri and Aqua left the JSDF Messland base at least six hours ago, weapons in hand and ready. The Super Soldier checked the GPS and showed his captain that they were getting close to the German-Messland-Netherlands border.

"Excellent," said Yuri as he held the GPS in his hand. He checked the time on his watch. "Coming up to 11:30 pm."

Aqua nodded at hearing the time. "Night's still young."

Out of nowhere, they were both hit with a cold snap. They've reached the Arctic borders.

"Since when was it THIS cold?" asked Yuri, shocked by how cold it just got.

"That means we're close to the Wraith," said Aqua, in an informative matter-of-fact tone.

Yuri had a flashback of when the Wraith attacked him at the hospital. He remembered it got strangely colder the further down the elevator went. Then, after the Wraith pounced on him, it went black from there. He then remembered when the Wraith jumped out at Greene, Crimson, and him from the time he was held in a dungeon with the two.

"… yep, got it, lad," Yuri said, in a rushed and fast-paced tone of voice.

Aqua turned on the helicopter's beam light. "Go for it. Take control of the light and try to spot the snow castle."

He nodded, then leapt into the cockpit of the helicopter and took control of the co-pilot beam-light. He used it to scan the area that they were flying over. After a little bit of searching, Yuri faced him.

"Nothing," said Yuri.

"Don't give up. Here, try to find ice too," Aqua responded. "And as 'well-no-shit' as this sounds, look for something that doesn't look naturally made."

Yuri rolled his eyes, unamused, and resumed control of the beam-light. He shone the light on the lower ground and eventually found a single-story snow and ice-looking structure.

"I think I found it," Yuri spoke.

"Excellent!" exclaimed Aqua. "Let's have a look."

Yuri nodded. "All right, but maybe try to land somewhere that's not around the structure, in case the Wraith catches on."

Aqua gave a thumbs up. "Good thinking." He started to steer the helicopter a bit away from the snowy structure. He landed at the opposite end of the mountain from the snowy structure.

"Why here?" Yuri inquired. "Won't we have to climb a mountain?"

"That's the neat part," Aqua responded.

They both get out of the cockpit, and Aqua walks towards a very specific part of the mountainside.

"Lucky for us, there's a one-way tunnel between this mountain," Aqua said. "When you shone that beam of light, I saw an opening on the side of the mountain. It doesn't take a genius to figure out it's a tunnel."

Yuri snorted. "It could also be an opening to a mine," he said as he got closer to Aqua. He hit Yuri over the arm. Yuri recoiled in a bit of pain.

"You're funny, you know that?" Aqua said teasingly as he stepped into the tunnel.

The captain took a second to recover before he followed Aqua into the tunnel. The light from the blaster rifle lit up the immediate area, making navigation a bit easier for both of them. Both men eventually make it to the other side and are met with a few spruce trees. They step through the spruce bushland and are face-to-face with the single-story ice building, with empty window frames. It looked a bit like an assembly hall, except no furniture in sight. It was the entrance.

Yuri eyed past the entrance. It was a large, icy hallway leading to a throne. He spotted the Wraith, floating above a golden throne. Yuri also spotted a familiar figure…

"Is that…" he stammered as he eyed the figure.

"Is… what?" inquired Aqua cautiously, looking over at Yuri. Concern was heard in his voice.

Yuri could feel himself having a flashback. He realised that it was the android that killed Jackson. And now, in person, it was holding a long crimson blade, and under the Wraith's command.

He sighed and calmed down. "Don't worry about it," he said to Aqua as he readied his submachine guns.

Aqua looked over at Yuri, shrugged, and readied his blaster rifle. "Ok then," he said.

Captain Yuri looked at the entrance of the snowy structure, then back at Aqua. "How are we supposed to go in?" he asked.

Aqua looked at the entrance to the structure, then back at Yuri, then the structure, then back at him once more. "We could do in with two methods: stealth, or guns blazing."

The captain pondered for a bit, then looked right into the

glowing eye sockets of Aqua's helmet. "I actually have an idea myself."

"Oh?" he asked curiously. "And what's that?"

"Ok, you go in sneaky, and I go in and cause a bit of a distraction," said Yuri.

Aqua nodded along with Yuri's plan. "Sounds good to me," he said, followed by a satisfactory shrug.

And thus, Yuri stepped to the left side of the entrance, and Aqua snuck to the right. The captain peeked over to try and see what the Wraith was doing. It looked to be in its own world, not even paying attention, like it wasn't even conscious at that point in time. Typical for something that's technically undead. The android turned towards the Wraith, sword in hand. It also looked not to care. This was a perfect vulnerable point. A vulnerability that both Yuri and Aqua could easily exploit. The Super Soldier snuck around the corner and started to stealthily make his way behind the entrance of what appeared to be the throne room, whatever it was. The JSDF captain looked over at him and awaited a silent signal of 'go ahead.' Aqua noticed this and gave him a thumbs up, then regripped his blaster rifle, tight in his grip.

Yuri gave Aqua a nod before he dashed out from behind the entrance to the snowy structure and slid down the icy floor. Gradually losing speed and approaching a thick, snowy slab, he leapt out and landed behind the left throne room entrance.

The Wraith took quick notice of the movement and faced

where Yuri had just hidden behind. It slowly started to float toward where Yuri was. He leapt out and aimed both MP7 submachine guns, one pointed at the Wraith and the other at the android. He was fully exposed, in contrast to Aqua, who was still hidden. The Wraith let out its signature high-pitched lunar-sounding screech, its arms outstretched.

Yuri glanced at the MP7 in his right hand and back at the Wraith. Aqua watched, blaster rifle ready. The Wraith used its phantom-like abilities to summon a large faceless humanoid figure, made entirely from snow. Yuri aimed both weapons at the large snow figure and took a deep breath. The android snuck behind the snow and gold throne as the large snowman stepped toward Yuri. It looked like it was around three to five metres tall, probably four. He charged at the snowman. It lifted its large leg, clearly about to do a stomp attack. Yuri took notice and got ready to enact a power slide move. He slid against the ground, completing a full-on power slide, narrowly dodging the stomp attack from the snow golem. Yuri leapt up and shot multiple rounds at the back of the golem's head. The golem fell to its knees. The Wraith, furious, lunged at Yuri. He leapt toward the side. He narrowly avoided the Wraith's attack. Yuri got to his feet and held his forehead. He face-planted. The Wraith saw this opportunity and flew toward Yuri again. He leaned backwards, and the Wraith was outside of the snowy structure. The golem slowly melted. The Wraith attempted one more flight attack, of which Yuri moved to the side subconsciously.

"Too close..." Yuri said, exhausted, as he took some time

to recover. He was strong, yes, but this match-up wasn't looking super good.

A large deep blue sphere overtook The Wraith, enveloping it completely. When the sphere disappeared, it was nowhere to be seen. Yuri looked around for the Wraith, confused as to where it disappeared. The throne room was not big by any means, so it should've been easy to find The Wraith's location. Yuri stepped towards where it just was.

"Where did that damn phantom go?" Yuri asked to himself.

With no warning, the Wraith appeared right behind him. It slowly floated toward Yuri, making no noise at all. All Yuri could hear was the sound of the snowy winds outside. He knew Aqua was going to intervene soon.

The Wraith, being close to Yuri now, shoved him down to the ground, and summoned some ice. The captain was pinned to the ground with ice, his hands and feet frozen. Yuri tilted his head and saw his MP7 submachine guns in his hands, also frozen by the ice. He saw the Wraith move to the corner of the room, by the throne room exit. The android leapt out from behind the throne itself, doing multiple front flips mid-air. After it landed, the android moved toward Yuri as if it were on roller skates. The floor, being slippery, made skating like that possible. The android gripped the large crimson blade in both hands and lifted it up. The blade was facing down at Yuri. It was going to stab him.

"Oh, shit…" murmured Yuri. This was the end, he thought. The end of the ever-so-scalding battle.

Out of nowhere, a random soldier lunged through the hollow window and tackled the android. The soldier gripped the torso of the android, landing on top of it. Being unarmed, he slapped the android across the face. The android shoved the soldier off. He did a backflip and landed again, and the android stood up completely. Its sword sliced the soldier's head off, his head falling onto the ground and rolling past Yuri.

The captain was still stuck helplessly on the floor. The android turned its attention toward him and slowly approached. It put the tip of the blade against Yuri's chest, ready to push down at any time and finally put an end to the captain. The Wraith watched as the android did this, its cold, emotionless face watching the android get ready to lay waste to Yuri. Though not doing anything, it wouldn't be too far-fetched to believe that The Wraith was amused.

Suddenly, Aqua revealed himself. He stood in the centre of the entrance and aimed his blaster rifle at the throne itself, intending to burn down the entire throne room.

"Go to hell, you skeletal freak!" yelled Aqua through his helmet.

The Wraith and the Android looked at Aqua, but they were too late. He pulled the trigger. A ton of energy started to surround the barrel of the rifle, circling around it like an aura of sorts. After just two seconds, the energy was released. It fired like a massive laser. The light from the energy was blinding. It was white and very bright yellow, just like the LED lighting on the blaster rifle.

BURNING PALACE

The captain woke up with ringing ears. He looked around for a bit and realised that the whole structure was in flames. Aqua picked him up and dashed him out. He was still holding both MP7 submachine guns, and the Super Soldier had his blaster rifle on his back as if it were a sword.

"Thanks for coming back for me," whispered Yuri with exhaustion present in his tone and facial expression.

"It's the least I could do," Aqua responded as he turned around and looked toward the exit of the burning structure.

The captain spotted the android, caught in the flames, slowly burning from within. The Wraith, however, was nowhere to be seen. Both soldiers knew it would've teleported away. Aqua carried Yuri out of the burning structure and placed him on the grass outside as Yuri recovered from almost being caught in the laser's fire and being blown up, too. It was guaranteed that the android would burn with the castle, ceasing to exist.

The next day, he woke up in the Messland JSDF base's infirmary. It was a rather small infirmary, with the basic wards and beeping machines. In a way, it was basically a small hospital, with the essentials.

"Hey, Yuri. Welcome back!" exclaimed Aqua, still wearing the armour Yuri had come to be familiar with.

"… you say that like I was on the verge of death," Yuri responded as he stood up from the bed.

"I know," Aqua teased. "But in a way, you kind of were."

Yuri looked over at the clock on the wall. It read 23:42 pm.

"Is it seriously that late?" asked Yuri.

"What? Eleven at night?" Aqua questioned, following up on Yuri's question.

"Yeah," he responded.

Aqua laughed right in front of him. He walked over to the infirmary door, beckoning Aqua to follow behind.

As they both walked down the corridor, Yuri looked over at Aqua.

"The burning palace… was that your blaster rifle then?" he asked with curiosity.

He looked over at Yuri and chuckled. "Oh, yes, that was

the rifle right," he said, then burst into a fit of laughter.

"You laugh a lot," Yuri responded, not very amused. He was more serious if anything.

Aqua laughed again. "I know."

Both of the soldiers arrived at the sleeping quarters of the base. Yuri took off his blue captain coat and his black captain cap, now only wearing his white singlet, brown long pants, heavy-duty black boots and black fingerless gloves. Aqua stepped over to the furthest bed and laid down on it.

"You're going to wear your armour to bed then?" Yuri asked, finding a bit of humour in this.

"Yep," Aqua responded.

Yuri chuckled. "Oh my god."

DOMAINS

The following morning, Yuri woke up early. He checked the time with the clock on the wall. 5:36 am. He got up, slipped on his boots, sprayed some deodorant, slipped on his jacket, slapped on his hat, and picked up both of his MP7 submachine guns.

Aqua got up shortly after. He grabbed his blaster rifle from the side and walked over to Captain Yuri.

"Morning cap'," said Aqua.

He looked over at his American ally and gave a quick good morning back.

They both arrived at the base's cafeteria a bit late. Breakfast had already been put out by the chefs. Yuri looked over at Aqua.

"Guess they beat us to it, huh," he said.

Aqua nodded. "Yep."

"I'm not really that hungry this morning," Yuri said as he poured himself a double shot of espresso coffee. "You, however, feel free to help yourself."

He raised an eyebrow behind his helmet but shrugged shortly after. "I'm still good as well."

Yuri looked over at Aqua. "Should we get going then?" he asked as he glanced over at the door.

The two walked down the corridor, weapons in hand. Yuri was taking Aqua to the depot.

"So, for today's mission, we're going to need a van."

Aqua looked over at Yuri. "Wait, why?" he asked.

Yuri pulled out his phone and showed Aqua a Telegram message. "One of our other more secretive spies informed us of one of the Wraith's domains," he said as he scrolled down, showing a picture.

Aqua looked over at the picture on the screen.

"This is where a former soldier and I fought a big crystal-ee golem. Legends call it: *The Temple of Hell…* as lame as that name is," Yuri explained

Aqua raised an eyebrow. He took the phone out of his hands and got a better look at the image.

"Damn me if I'm wrong," said Aqua, "but isn't this one of the many ancient temples in European folklore?" he asked.

Yuri looked over at him.

"Yes, *The Temple of Hell* is one of the many ancient temples. I'm not big on history by any means, but I'm pretty sure legend claims this temple used to send people directly to hell… at least as far as legend goes."

He unlocked the van and climbed into the driver's seat. "Aqua, get in. We're going on a road trip. There are two backpacks, one for each of us. Each backpack contains a compass, a map of Messland, and two bottles of water."

Aqua climbed into the passenger seat and looked back, discovering the two backpacks Yuri was talking about.

"Oh, by the way," Aqua said. "There's a blacksmith on the route to the temple."

He pulled out his blaster rifle, revealing it was a bit worn out.

"These things may be cool as hell; however, they are prone to breaking. I know how to fix them, and we should stop at a blacksmith so I can make some repairs," Aqua explained as he rubbed one of the busted areas over the blaster rifle.

In understanding, Yuri nodded. "Very well, we'll make a pitstop for repairs."

"Thank you," Aqua said.

THROUGH THE VALLEYS

The van drove through the valleys. Aqua had his head sticking out the window, obviously still in his gear. Yuri was the one driving the van. He knew the way to the temple, knowing the route from his previous trip there with Jackson. Despite using a different route previously, Yuri knew what to look for.

"This trip is boring," Aqua whined.

He plugged in an FM transmitter to his phone, connected it to the van's radio, and turned on some heavy metal and rock music. Yuri took notice.

"What are you doing?" he asked as the sound of blaring guitars filled the van.

"Making this trip less dull," Aqua responded.

Captain Yuri face palmed, but appreciated the gesture from his American ally, making the trip in the van a lot less awkward and quiet.

"There it is!" exclaimed Aqua.

Yuri pulled to the side of the road, in front of a brick structure. It was two stories high, had light grey bricks made from stone as the roof, and looked a bit like it was built in the Middle Ages, with all the stone brick décor around the exterior of the building. In front of the structure was a shoveled path, and near the brick building was a wooden scaffold, likely for a second building.

"Are you sure this is the blacksmith?" asked Yuri, looking over at Aqua.

"This is it, alright," he responded, then got out of the van, blaster rifle in hand.

He had no choice but to trust Aqua on his declaration. Yuri got out of the driver's seat and followed his ally to the door. Aqua opened the door and walked over to the anvil. The floorboards were made from wooden planks, and so were the stairs that went up to the 2nd floor. The first floor was lit up with a gas lantern, the type used on camping trips. The captain noticed a storage chest and opened it. Inside were a few pieces of metal, some nails, and a hammer.

"Do you want these?" he asked as he placed his MP7s to the side and picked up what he found in the chest.

Aqua looked over and nodded. "Yeah, pass 'em here," he said.

He got closer to Yuri and took the tools out of his hands. Aqua stepped back to the anvil and began work. The captain picked up his MP7s again.

It had been a couple of hours since they both arrived at the blacksmith building, which was located in the middle of nowhere for whatever reason. Aqua had been hard at work fixing his blaster rifle while Yuri sat down and processed everything. From the first time he was enlisted in the JSDF, to becoming the captain, to fighting the red crystalised golem, to watching Jackson get mutilated right in front of him, he thought of it all.

He snapped out of his daze when the door opened. The soldiers looked over at the open door, and someone he definitely was not expecting walked in. It was Greene.

Aqua looked over at Yuri, who looked a bit agitated now. He put down the hammer and stepped closer to Yuri.

"Came back for more?" he growled as he stepped closer to Greene.

"Relax, I'm turning myself in!" said Greene.

He stepped closer to Yuri, arms raised in the air. He got on his knees. Was Greene really surrendering himself? Yuri went from angry to sceptical. He aimed his right MP7 at Greene.

"I can explain everything!" he followed up with in desperation.

"… come with me," Yuri said.

He walked up the stairs, expecting Greene to follow behind. Aqua followed behind Greene, making sure he would not try to escape. The second story had beds in it. One in each corner, some in the middle, and a few by the railing where the stairs were. The plank flooring also remained. The room was lit up with a gas lantern. Between the beds in the middle was a bookshelf, though mostly empty. The few books that were on the shelf were '*To Kill A Mockingbird*,' '*Tomorrow, When The War Began*,' '*Pride and Prejudice*,' and '*1984*.' Aqua saw the titles on the bookshelf and chuckled to himself.

"Whoever was here last must really like their books," he said, then snapped out of his laughter shortly after noticing Yuri starting to interrogate Greene.

"Why are you here?" asked Yuri, a bit irritated, but keeping a professional tone of voice.

"I killed Crimson."

Yuri tensed up. He wasn't afraid, but he was confused. And still sceptical. He got his act together shortly after though.

"What do you mean you *killed* Crimson?" he asked.

"Let me explain," said Greene, looking around the room, then back at Yuri. He sighed, closed his eyes, and resumed talking.

"Me and him were fighting The Wraith. Crimson spilt

gasoline everywhere and threw a box of matches at me. He yelled at me to light a match to try to burn it to death. I took a match out of the box, lit it, and threw it into the gasoline."

Greene had started to tense up a bit. He thought he was oversharing, but he didn't want to die as well.

"And then?" asked Yuri.

"Well, we didn't realise it, but Crimson was in the gasoline too. I threw the match, then quickly realised my mistake. It was too late. He was in flames, and The Wraith warped away before the flames got it. Crimson burned alive and I was helpless. All I could do was watch."

Yuri let out a whistle at what Greene said.

"Bloody hell…" murmured Aqua.

While they were all discussing, they heard a high-pitched, lunar-sounding screech. Yuri glanced out the window, and Aqua peeked out from behind him. They saw The Wraith floating above a small pond, under one hundred metres away from the blacksmith. Instantly, the building went silent.

"What do we do?" whispered Aqua.

"We get the hell out of here," Yuri responded.

They both dashed downstairs. Aqua grabbed his blaster rifle and Yuri reloaded both his MP7s.

"What about me?" asked Greene.

"What about you?" asked Yuri, a stern tone filling his voice.

"You can't just leave me here to die!" Greene exclaimed. For the first time, Yuri saw fear. Fear, in a terrorist. Aqua snorted at the fear in Greene's expression and tone of voice.

"Murderers like you are irredeemable," Yuri said in response, then turned to the Super Soldier. "Come on, let's go. We can attempt an ambush against The Wraith at the temple."

Aqua nodded and followed Yuri out of the blacksmith and back into the van.

"Wait, but Doomo was decapitated and Crimson is dead. I have nobody. And if my bosses find out I failed my goal..." Greene realised his pleas were pathetic, as neither soldier listened.

Yuri got into the driver's seat, and Aqua got into the passenger seat. He slammed on the pedal, and the van sped off, away from the blacksmith. Aqua looked into the reflective mirror on the side of the van and saw The Wraith using some sort of glowing blue psychic ray attack against the blacksmith. The building froze over entirely. He looked closer and saw Greene freeze to death inside the building, helpless to stop it.

"Damn..." he murmured, shuddering at the sight.

THE TEMPLE OF HELL

Speeding off into a thunderstorm, the skies overhead the valley got significantly darker. The van was speeding at a very swift pace, almost like its own grey blur. Fog blanketed the surrounding area, and the mountains were barely visible. Yuri was fully concentrated on getting to *The Temple of Hell* by any means necessary. Aqua kept the heavy metal music pumping. The captain was starting to get a bit agitated.

"Aqua, it's great you have good taste in music, but please turn it down so I don't get distracted, crash into a tree, and kill both of us," he said, trying to keep calm as he swerved around trees, bushes, and tall patches of grass.

He sighed, but gave in to Yuri's request. He turned off the music and disconnected his FM transmitter. The captain let out a breath of relief as he continued driving, his eyes concentrated on the valley ahead of him, being careful not to crash. A lightning bolt flashed across and struck the grass right in front of the van. Yuri panicked and lost control of the vehicle. It spun out. Desperate, Aqua grabbed the wheel in an attempt to help his Japanese ally avoid crashing into a tree. To their luck, they avoided hitting a tree or crashing into a ditch.

"Ok, let's agree to be a bit slower," said Aqua as he let out a sigh of relief behind his helmet.

Yuri nodded. "Yeah, good idea."

The rest of the van trip was uneventful, minus a few lightning strikes barely missing the van. Yuri managed to remain calm as he drove the van and narrowly dodged lightning strikes. They arrived at *The Temple Of Hell* and stepped out of the vehicle. Yuri felt a bit anxious inside, but he swallowed his fear down. He couldn't afford to let his fear own him. Not at a crucial time. Aqua's emotion was hidden from view, but from the looks of it, he seemed brave.

"So… are we ready?" asked Yuri.

Aqua looked over at Yuri, blaster rifle in hand, and nodded. "Yeah, I think we are."

He took his two MP7s off his waistbelt, holding one in each hand. This was the moment where the fate of Messland lay in the hands (and weapons) of two brave soldiers.

Captain Yuri was the first to enter the temple. He walked with side steps, pointing his right MP7 in front of him, the left submachine gun to his side. Aqua followed behind slowly, blaster rifle in grip as he slowly stepped. There was only one way out: through the temple.

Inside *The Temple of Hell*, it was boiling hot. Yuri had forgotten how hot the temple really was, only remembering how hot it could get after walking right into the entrance. He made it to the other end with minimal issues.

"Man, it gets hot in this armour," said Aqua, a bit feebly but hanging in there.

"You're telling me…" he spoke, starting to sweat a bit, even in his coat. "No wonder this temple got the name it did."

The Super Soldier let out a small whistle, then looked to his right, where he saw crumbled pillars. Yuri looked over to his right as well.

"Oh, no way…" he murmured.

All the pillars had collapsed.

"… now what?" said Yuri, following up with what he just said.

"I guess we'll just have to…" Aqua murmured before pointing his blaster rifle at the wall to the left of the obstacle course.

"No, don't!" yelled Yuri, desperation in his tone. "That blaster rifle of yours. It probably won't be strong enough to withstand a second attack against The Wraith," he pointed out.

Aqua looked down at his blaster rifle. He inspected it, then let out a small, defeated sigh. "Alright… No destruction for now."

The captain sighed in relief.

"We'll have to find another way over this course, though," Aqua said as he looked at the gaping lava pit. "If we need to get through to the other side, we need to get past."

"To fight off and kill The Wraith," Yuri followed up with.

"Yeah…"

As if Aqua's words were magic, the entire temple suddenly experienced a cold snap. All the sweat Yuri and Aqua accumulated turned to small shards of ice that fell right down. Additionally, the lava pit froze over, and so did the flowing lava. It was all iced over. The Wraith was nearby.

"At least we aren't going to die of heat stroke anymore," Yuri said after a small piece of silence.

"Oh, yeah," Aqua responded. "It's *The Temple of Freeze* now," he remarked.

The two walked over the frozen-over obstacle course. It was a bit more like an ice rink now. Yuri took careful steps over the ice while Aqua wasted no time and slid on the ice as if he were really ice skating. Though he could only slide, due to his armour and weapon, Aqua still found a way to make it fun. Yuri watched as Aqua skied by, a hint of a laid-back and soft small smile on his face.

Both men made it to the other side of the course with minimal disruption. They both looked to the left, where the arena was in sight. And there it was: the Wraith. It was right there, floating, facing the back wall.

THE MOST INTENSE BATTLE YET

"Well…" spoke Yuri. "Keep your distance."

Aqua nodded, acceptingly. He knew that keeping a safe distance would be a smart idea. Dying was not on his to-do list anytime soon by any means, so staying away from The Wraith it was.

Inside the dark brick arena was a large red crystalised spire, where the golem was slain, as well as a few craters in the ground. The large spire reached the tips of the walls in the arena in height. It also pulsed similar energy to that of the big red crystal golem. Maybe the golem's remains became the spire…

Yuri was the first one to walk. In the same stance, he was when entering *The Temple of Hell.* He started the treacherous, slow walk toward The Wraith, who seemingly hadn't noticed them just yet. The captain continued to walk slowly toward The Wraith, with the MP7 in his right hand, pointing directly at its head. Aqua had started to walk slowly behind Yuri. It felt as though time itself had frozen over. Nothing but the deafening sound of silence remained to keep the footsteps on the dark grey brick tiles company, aside from a few of the evening bird chirps.

The distance between the soldiers and The Wraith grew shorter and shorter. Soon enough, the distance was that of ten metres. It turned around and faced both Yuri and Aqua. It let out its typical high-pitched lunar-like screech before a large, glowing blue sphere surrounded it, the transparency turning into a solid shade of deep blue. Yuri and Aqua turned to face each other, then took a few steps back. The blue ball grew to be three times bigger before it faded away. In front of the men stood an entirely different creature.

It had a light blue icy body, a long neck, a long tail, two wings, one front leg in the middle of the body, two back legs, and no eyes to be seen. The bottom parts of the leg were a crystallised dark blue, as long as the wing structure. The new beast had a jaw and only two large upper canine teeth. It shared the dark blue hood, except this hood was crystallised too. Both men looked at the new beast, horrified.

"Got a fancy name for this one?" asked Aqua. His voice was slightly shuddering. Nobody could have predicted *this*.

"The Spectral," replied Captain Yuri.

The creature, known now as The Spectral, let out a similar-sounding cry that The Wraith had previously, except the frequencies sounded different, and it was longer. The skies overhead turned a darker blue, and the clouds turned a very light shade of blue. The temperature got significantly colder.

Though it had no eyes, it looked down at both the men. Both Yuri and Aqua knew this was going to be the most intense battle yet. No matter what, they knew this was not going to be easy by any means, with just the two of them.

"We got this," spoke Yuri bravely. He held both MP7 submachine guns out, aiming at The Spectral.

Aqua aimed his blaster rifle at the neck of the beast and nodded in silence as he got ready to fire. The beast let out its high-pitched lunar cry, then looked down at them more intently. It slowly started to approach Aqua, prompting Yuri to fire some shots to distract it. The bullets from the rapidly firing submachine guns struck its neck. Promptly, The Spectral turned its attention to Yuri and growled.

The captain was the first to make an actual offensive attack. With more agility than he had, Yuri ran up the arena wall, performed a backflip, and fired some shots at The Spectral. It was buffeted and let out a small hiss, but it was still standing.

"Nice shots!" exclaimed Aqua.

The Spectral stepped towards Aqua and spun around. It was trying to strike the American Super Soldier with its tail. When its tail was about to hit Aqua, he ducked. The large blue tail flew over Aqua's head. The Spectral then leaned down and tried to crunch down on Aqua. He held out his blaster rifle. The blaster was now between The Spectral's jaws. It picked up Aqua, who was dangling and holding onto his weapon for dear life. Bravely, he pulled the trigger. Pulling the trigger made an explosion occur in The Spectral's mouth, and it screeched out in pain as Aqua began his descent. Yuri spotted his ally falling down and leapt forward to break Aqua's fall.

"Thanks for that just now," said Aqua in response.

"Any time," Yuri responded.

They both got to their feet, and Yuri fired more shots at The Spectral. It let out another growl in pain.

Out of nowhere, an African-American man leapt down and slashed at The Spectral's neck with two knives, and then landed in front of it.

The new man wore a white singlet, black long pants and white joggers, as well as a white sweatband. He was a similar height to both Yuri and Aqua.

"No time to explain," the man said.

Without warning, the crystal spire started to glow a bit. All three men faced the spire and raised an eyebrow. The glow went from the base of the spire to the spire's tip. Out of nowhere, a ton of lasers fired everywhere across the arena. All the men dodged the lasers, narrowly. The Spectral let out an intense and loud roar of pain.

Aqua winced at the sound of the screech and accidentally

fired his blaster rifle. The energy started building up, and it swiftly fired directly at The Spectral's front leg. It disintegrated upon impact with the laser. It was now standing upright. It let out a loud screech of pain, mixed with the sounds of a loud roar.

"Jesus, does that thing make a new sound with every incident?" asked Aqua, still a bit shaken from the roar previously.

"Probably… but that's not relevant!" Yuri shouted in response.

The Spectral – now standing upright – stepped towards all three men, its tail swishing around and its wings stretched outward. All three men backed up a bit. Aqua attempted to fire another shot from his blaster rifle at The Spectral but was met with a click from his weapon, followed by the barrel starting to smoke a bit.

"Damnit…" he murmured, looking down at his rifle.

The crystalised spire fired another round of lasers in random directions. The men dodged the new round. One of the lasers hit Yuri's left MP7, melting it to the point where not even ashes remained.

"Shit…" he cursed under his breath while clenching both fists.

Though Yuri still had one MP7 in his right hand, he was still a bit salty that he lost one of his guns to the lasers.

The African-American tapped Yuri's shoulder. Both men

glanced over at The Spectral. Aqua caught wind of this too. The Spectral had lost both legs and was now purely airborne, though it stayed above the arena floor, and not leaving the structure at all. The laser must've melted The Spectral's two back legs.

"By the way, my name's Gamma," said the African-American. "Unusual name, I know, but I think this is the best time to introduce myse-"

Gamma was cut off by The Spectral, letting out a loud and high-pitched screech.

"I'm Yuri, and that's Aqua," said Yuri in response, in a fast-paced tone of voice.

He gave a hand movement, like "what's up," before he ran toward The Spectral. Yuri held his MP7 aimed at the monster. Aqua sat against the wall, hammer and wrench in hand, trying to fix his weapon as fast as possible, trying not to sell the mission.

Captain Yuri fired a few more shots at The Spectral's face, just above his jaw. Gamma spotted a strange, small, and deep blue crystal at the back of The Spectral's head. He knew that was its weak point. He ran up the wall that the beast was facing away from and did a front flip onto its back. Before Gamma could get close, The Spectral's tail grabbed a grip of him like a snake constricting its prey. He stabbed and sliced at the tail, hoping to get out. But he was unsuccessful. Yuri recognised the trouble his new ally was in and fired shots at The Spectral's lower jaw, around its neck area. It screeched in pain, then let go of Gamma. He used his knives like icebreakers and stabbed into the side of The Spectral's body. The blade slid down the side of its body, creating a wide gap in it. Blood flew swiftly, gushing out as Gamma fell. He landed on both feet and dashed back to Yuri and Aqua as The Spectral roared out in pain.

"Thanks," he said.

Yuri nodded at Gamma in approval. He dashed back under The Spectral and performed a wall run at the far back wall again. This time, however, the beast was disoriented. Now was his chance. Gamma landed on the back of the monster once more. It tried to shake him off but failed due to its disorientated state. Gamma stabbed its back and crawled forward, stabbing it in the back more, like an ice hiker climbing up, or a rock climber scaling a mountain.

Eventually, Gamma reached The Spectral's neck. He scaled up its neck, still in rock climber fashion. Yuri and Aqua took notice of what his new ally was doing.

"I don't believe it…" murmured Aqua as he looked up at Gamma, taken away from his work.

"No way…" Yuri murmured in response.

With a determined attitude, Gamma sliced the crystal at the back of The Spectral's head, destroying it in just a few slices. The Spectral roared in pain. Its roar echoed throughout the arena and likely around the surrounding area too. Its body started falling toward the ground. Gamma kept one of his knives in the back of its neck, holding on tight to not lose his balance and experience a nasty fall.

203

RELIEF

Gamma was the first to wake up. His knives were out of his grip, resting on the deep grey brick tile ground nearby.

The skies overhead had now turned back to the blue they were used to, and the clouds had become clear and white once more. The sun was shining super brightly in the sky. It must be a new day.

He sat up and glanced around, leaning back on his hands. The man saw Yuri lying by the hollow entrance. He just assumed that the captain was unconscious. The collision was big, after all. Gamma then saw The Spectral's corpse, by the far left of the arena. His eyes then laid on Aqua, who was unconscious against the far left wall of the arena. He got up and grabbed his knives from the ground. He held them in his left hand and walked over to Aqua first.

Aqua had started to stir up a bit while unconscious. He was going to wake up soon. Gamma figured he'd have to take Aqua's helmet off so the cool air could get to it. He put both knives down and started to try and remove Aqua's helmet but to no avail. He made a second attempt but failed. After a few more attempts, Gamma let out a defeated groan of annoyance.

"Damn, what is this thing made of?" he asked himself as he looked down at the yet-to-be-conscious Aqua.

Aqua woke up on his own and was met with Gamma the first person he saw. He held out his hand for Aqua to grab onto. He grabbed Aqua's hand and pulled him up.

"Thank you," said Aqua weakly.

"It's ok," Gamma responded.

Aqua hoisted his blaster rifle over his back and looked over at Yuri. Gamma also looked over at him too.

"Is he alright?" asked Aqua before he walked over.

He sprinted past Aqua and held Yuri in his free hand. The back of Yuri's head was in Gamma's hand. He was out cold. Aqua had just caught up to the African-American who had just saved both their lives and looked down at Yuri's limp body.

"God damn…" murmured Aqua through his helmet.

He removed the armour on both of his hands and placed his right hand on Yuri's forehead. It was cold. Stiff. Aqua moved his hand to the captain's chest. There was a steady heartbeat. Though unconscious, he was at least relaxed.

"I found a heartbeat," Aqua said to Gamma.

He let out the biggest sigh of relief, then turned to Aqua.

"Do you have any way to contact the JSDF?" asked Gamma. "We might be able to get a helicopter ride out of here."

Aqua looked over at Gamma.

"Yes, perfect idea!" exclaimed Aqua. "I have means of contacting the base."

He took Yuri's portable radio from his belt and turned it on. He switched the nuzzle to the JSDF private radio network and spoke into the device.

"We need an airlift. This is Aqua, Yuri's deployed ally. We're in the arena inside *The Temple Of Hell.*"

After a few seconds, a voice crackled through the radio's speaker.

"Deployed. Take care of yourselves. Over."

This was amazing news. They hadn't been left for dead after all.

"Ok, you take Yuri's wrists, and I'll take his legs. We'll move him to the centre of the arena," ordered Aqua as he grabbed Yuri's legs.

Gamma nodded, tossed his knives to the side, and grabbed Yuri's wrists. They both coordinated his body to the centre of the arena and carefully placed him down on the cold dark grey brick-tiled floor. The centre was next to a crater.

Not long after placing the captain's body down, Aqua spoke up.

"How did you know we needed help?" he asked.

Gamma chuckled softly to himself, then started to explain. "I saw your van drive past my valley. From the near misses, the thunderbolts, and figuring out where you were headed. It wasn't too farfetched to know you two were going to The Temple of Hell."

He continued to explain as Aqua intently listened.

"Knowing the dangers that The Temple of Hell faces, I decided to follow your van. I was originally going to check to make sure you guys were not digging your own graves. After a while, I saw you guys fighting The Wraith, and I just had to step in."

Aqua nodded. The story definitely matched up, after all. "Well, thanks for looking out for two strangers."

"It's no problem," Gamma responded.

AIR SUPPORT

Half an hour passed by. The air support Aqua called in could be heard above them, slowly descending. Slowly, the helicopter got closer, and closer, and closer, all until they were right above the arena. Aqua looked up and saw the helicopters. A rope was propelled down as the helicopter slowly made its descent, making sure the rope could be reached. At the bottom of the rope was a small footing pad. Aqua held Yuri in one arm and the rope in the other, and stepped onto the footing pad. It ascended up into the air toward the helicopter. Holding both the rope and Yuri tight in his hands, Aqua did not look down at the ground below as the rope continued its ascension.

Eventually, they reached the helicopter. Aqua threw Yuri inside the helicopter and then pulled himself over. After that, the helicopter took off.

As the helicopter flew overhead the Alps, Aqua realised something: he had forgotten all about Gamma. It was too late. The helicopter had already departed. Sure, he just appeared and helped take out The Spectral, but he had the best agility. Even with all of that, he just forgot about Gamma. He took out a laptop from a port in the helicopter and started typing.

When the helicopter landed back at the JSDF Messland base, he wasted no time rushing the captain to the infirmary. The same one they were in not too long ago, when fighting the Wraith in the icy structure. As he ran through the halls, the captain in his arms, the passing-through faculty gave him weird looks. Nonetheless, Aqua rushed Yuri into the infirmary. He rushed through the stained glass door and dropped Yuri onto a bed. It was at that point that he woke up. Aqua was his first sight waking up. He couldn't remember a thing.

"What happened?" he asked.

"Long story short, I don't remember anything either," Aqua replied in response. "But we killed The Wraith, or The Spectral, or whatever history will remember it as."

Upon hearing Aqua confirm The Wraith was dead, Yuri let out the heaviest sigh of relief. The TV mounted to the infirmary wall switched to a breaking news report.

"Breaking news," spoke the reporter through the TV screen.

Both Yuri and Aqua look over at the TV, curious.

"Belarus has surrendered after its attack on Messland had gone horribly wrong. Just yesterday, a terrorist from Belarus was reported to have surrendered to the JSDF captain, named Yuri Katō."

Aqua looked over at Yuri, then back at the TV screen.

"Additionally, a JSDF recruit has confirmed that The Wraith is dead. He goes by Aqua. More on that later."

Weakly, Yuri moved his head to look at Aqua.

"You sly dog," he said casually, impressed with Aqua's sneaky movement.

Late-January 2027

REMEMBRANCE

It was midday and the skies were clear. In the Italian city of Palermo, Yuri held a private funeral for Jackson, in remembrance of his efforts against the Belarusian terrorists and The Wraith. One by one, Yuri's parents, Jackson's parents, a few of his cousins, Jackson's friends, Aqua, Gamma, and a few commanders and leaders in the JSDF, all turned up at the church. The parents, friends, and cousins were wearing black suits and dresses. The commanders and leaders were wearing formal uniforms. However, for everyone else in Messland and greater Europe, life went on as normally as possible. Recovery was going to be a long road, with a lot of effort required. But for most people, it was already underway. Some people may never recover, and that is normal. Some people would have life-long trauma. Some just wouldn't survive.

After giving his speech, the priest moved to the side, and Yuri stepped up to the lectern, piece of paper in hand. His expression was a bit deadpan, the distressed and worried kind. He placed the paper on the lectern and sighed. With a heavy heart, Yuri began to read from the paper on the lectern as he tried to avoid looking at the people who turned up.

"Today, we remember the life of Jackson Herehshie, a brave soldier from Saudi Arabia," spoke Yuri heavy-heartedly, his breath a bit shaky as he stuttered on a few words but no tears welled.

"He was a brave man, who fought alongside me against the Belarusian terrorists in Messland. He fought against The goddamn Wraith," he continued to speak.

"But most of all…" he murmured. "He was my friend."

Aqua and Gamma looked at each other, then back at Captain Yuri, who was still behind the lectern. He was trying to process his words.

"I don't have much else to say," said Yuri. "But I do miss him. I miss him dearly. I'll forever remember him."

He wrapped up and stepped to the side. Jackson's parents step up and start giving their speech too. Then his cousins. Then his friends. Then the commanders and leaders. Since Aqua and Gamma didn't actually meet Jackson, they didn't talk.

The funeral wrapped up after two hours. The commanders and leaders left the church. Everyone else stayed for the gathering.

THE BLUES OF WAR

The time was four in the morning. Yuri hadn't slept at all. With no sign of sleeping again for the rest of the night, Yuri got up and walked over to his kitchen. He got himself a glass of water and turned on the TV in his apartment's living room. He's had shadows around his eyes since watching his friend get murdered. Yuri had been spiralling psychologically since he won the battle against that monster.

Around a week after the funeral in January, Yuri was given $40,000 as a payout. Though he was fortunate, Yuri could not forget the sight of watching his best friend get stabbed in front of him, by a robot of all things.

The program on the TV was some rom-com from the 1950s. He wasn't bothered to find out the name of the show. The blues of war were just too much for Yuri's mind.

After thinking for a little while, he had an idea of what he could do that day.

"Maybe… I could go visit Jackson's grave," he thought, murmuring his thought out loud. "It's been a long while…"

The time had passed 10:00 am, and Yuri had not done a lot since he woke up around six hours ago. He got dressed into a plain blue hoodie – it was winter in Germany, where his apartment penthouse was – and black jeans. He also slipped on some white joggers. He paced outside and got into the utility truck that he purchased with some of the money donated to him by the JSDF itself.

The drive itself was just ten minutes. The streets weren't as crowded as Yuri thought they'd be. He parked in a parking lot not too far from the cemetery. Gloomy and grey clouds formed overhead as he walked across the road toward the cemetery's site. Before leaving, Yuri called the Messland JSDF base and completed his application for his regular service leave. He got twelve months on his leave.

Yuri stumbled into the cemetery site and looked around for a bit. As he slowly stumbled through the graveyard, he eyed the labels of graves. Some of the writing on the graves were faded out and weren't readable anymore. Some were hard to read, some were still fresh, and others had crumbled. He noticed a few of the graves written in different languages and dialects altogether. Yuri recognised a few of the languages – one was Arabic, one was Italian, one was Vietnamese, and one was even Korean. But he was only here for one reason only: Jackson.

After a while, he found Jackson's grave. A third was written in English (top half), the middle was in German, and the bottom was in Arabic. Yuri dug into his pocket and pulled out a green rose. He knew Jackson loved uniquely coloured flower petals; the type you'd expect to think didn't exist. He placed the rose in a small crack in the stone of his grave, the rose hanging over the crack, stuck in like a flower in a vase or pot.

Raindrops began to fall from the gloomy skies above. The word "alone" rang out through Yuri's mind. He was gone. Jackson was gone. Greene was gone. Crimson was gone. The Wraith/Spectral was (thankfully) gone. But now, Yuri was alone.

217

ACKNOWLEDGEMENTS + AUTHOR NOTES

Holy hell, this was one fun and ambitious story. Thank you all so much for reading my debut novel. I really had fun writing this, from the action to the heartbreak, to the action, and back to the heartbreak. You guys reading this at home made this all worth it to me and I could not thank you enough for giving this a chance.

Thank you to my awesome friend group (Isabelle Love, Sam Fox, Kelsey Henderson, Jackson Daley, Noah Tyler, Scotia Little, Raymond Butler, Jayde Pocock, Tiffany Hall, and Odele Rajkowski) for being there for me in times of tough!

Thank you a lot to my wonderful boyfriend Callum for being there at all times. Love you so much!

Thank you to Miss Lara Keller for giving the best constructive feedback and tips to improve my writing. She's an amazing English teacher and, honestly, most memorable if I'm being honest. Keep doing what you're doing!

Thank you to my cousin Bianca for being the sweetest cousin I've ever had (on my mum's side of the family), and thank you to Tristan for being the coolest cousin (on my dad's side). You two are both amazing.

Thank you to Michael Early and 'Wealth' for agreeing to become characters for this story (Michael is Aqua and Wealth is Gamma). To think we went from playing games together to effectively collaborating on a whole novel.

Thank you to David Laverick for supporting the idea for this novel and its many plots. Pull through, my friend.

Thank you to some of my other friends (Euan Bamford-Finnie, Oliver Bennett, Owen Rosengreen, and Lilianah K) for being there. You are all amazing as hell!

Thank you to Darcy Chalk for emotional support during the writing and especially editing of the book. Good luck with everything that life has to offer!

And thank you, reader, at home, for enjoying this story! Without you, this debut novel would be a waste of time for me to write personally. You all deserve a section here. Thanks again!

This book was written as a remake for the original Blues of War story. Blues of War was an animated series I made and posted on YouTube. It was a Minecraft animation because I was incapable of producing proper animations, and it was easier to complete. I operate two YouTube channels – one called 'Gold Productions' (handle is @goldproductionsog) and 'TooGold Productions' (handle is @TooGoldProductions).

If you would like to, please do consider checking out the channels. TooGold Productions is where my new videos go, and Gold Productions is my old channel, where you can find the show. The animation is horrible, looking back now, but it is the best way to find a visual version of the story. If this book performs really well, I might be able to remake the animated series too with a much higher budget. A guy can dream though.

If you enjoyed this novel, why not share it with a friend or two or encourage others to buy themselves a copy of the novel?

ABOUT THE AUTHOR

Cooper Gowell (penname is C.J. Gowell) is an author (more specifically, a self-published author), who's spent most of his life in a small rural town in Queensland, Australia. Wanting to be an author since year six (primary school), he started with writing (and forgetting about) a small, short story. Nowadays he works on novels while trying to not break under the pressure of getting older every year. There are many more stories on the way, with this debut novel being the gateway into a universe unlike any other.

If you meet me in public, please come and say hi. I promise, my social skills have gotten really good (I swear).